RIDORKULOUS

MARY FRAME

Cover design by Najla Qamber Designs
https://www.najlaqamberdesigns.com
Editing by Elizabeth Nover at Razor Sharp Editing
www.razorsharpediting.com

To all of my weirdos and geeks, nerds and dorks, the ones who hide and don't quite fit in, I see you.

You are my favorite <3

1

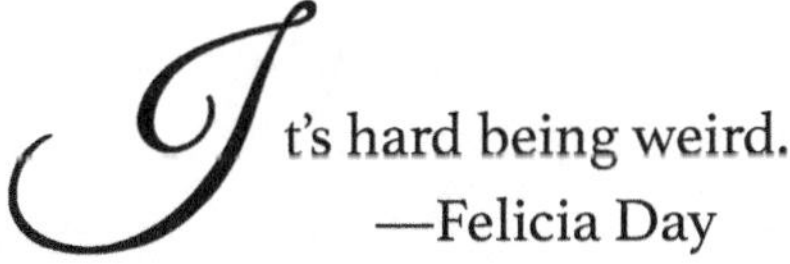

It's hard being weird.
—Felicia Day

Reese

Thump. Thump. Thump.

It's normal for my roommate's antics to wake me up in the dead of night.

Thump. Thump. Thump.

She's always noisy. Talking. Shrieking with her friends. Playing music too loud. Fooling around with a variety of jocks and frat boys. It's like she never sleeps. Since we became dormmates last year, I've adapted to the noise.

Thump. Thump. Thump.

Mostly.

Noise in the middle of the night . . . that is normal. What's not normal is my bed shaking in an unmistakable, rhythmic pattern.

The thick blanket over my head and noise-canceling headphones aren't going to be enough tonight, not when I'm being jostled awake.

Thump. Thump. Thump.

Even I can't pretend to ignore this. Slowly, I peer over the top of my comforter.

Abby's lamp on her nightstand is aglow, highlighting the top half of the room, but I can't see any signs of life from this vantage. Her bed is empty.

And yet *my* bed is still shaking.

Lifting my head a microinch, I search the rest of the room.

There. On the floor. The jerky movements belong to a large pair of Converses thrusting against the frame of my bed.

It must be Abby and . . . someone.

I don't recognize the guy on top.

All I can see is the back of a dark head. He's shirtless and his pants are halfway down his legs, bare bottom exposed. And hairy.

Ew.

I lower the blanket a little more, curiosity overwhelming the irritation and nervous flutters vying for my attention.

Are all guys so hairy? Do they all leave their pants

and shoes on when they engage in late-night dorm coitus?

More importantly, why can't Abby do this stuff on her own bed? Or better yet, somewhere far, far away.

I move one of the earpieces from my noise-canceling headphones and immediately regret it.

Loud moans emanate from the couple on the floor.

It's two o'clock in the morning. On a Tuesday. I have class in six hours.

Indecision and anxiety battle in my head. I can't lie here and watch, and I definitely can't sleep.

If I say something . . . Abby won't be happy. She already hates me. She loves to make my life hell and even though I try to ignore her, it's not easy.

If I interrupt their . . . whatever they're doing, she'll likely intensify her campaign to make me feel like the smallest life-form ever discovered, a nanobe of the lowest order.

Confrontation is not my thing. People in general aren't my thing. Especially when the people I need to speak with are naked and fornicating.

But before I can make a decision either way, there's a pounding on the door.

"Abby!" a masculine voice yells.

"Oh, shit," she hisses. "Get dressed!"

The figures on the floor scramble and yank clothes on and up, but they're too late.

The door flies open, slamming against the wall.

I flinch under the blanket but keep it low enough to continue watching.

I can't look away.

This is worse than a train wreck.

It's a made-for-TV movie where the train has been picked up by a tornado, thrown in with a shark, and destroyed by a bomb-wielding B-list actor.

Abby snaps her red satiny bra into place, and Hairy-Butt Man finally jerks his pants up over his rear.

"Are you kidding me?" The man in the doorway props an arm against the frame, supporting his long form, like he might crumple to the floor at any moment and this building is the only thing supporting him. His face is slack with disbelief.

I know him.

I mean, I know *of* him.

Fitz Moreland.

Abby's long-time boyfriend.

They've been together since birth or something.

And he's the "best boyfriend ever and will do anything and believe anything" according to Abby, who brags about their relationship to anyone who'll listen while simultaneously cheating on him nonstop.

I've never actually talked to Fitz Moreland or seen him this close up, despite the fact we are in our second year of college on the same campus in the same town less than a mile from where we all went to high school together.

I've always considered him attractive from afar, but up close it's even more obvious just how striking he is. He's the kind of handsome that kicks you right in the gut.

His hair is messy, longish, and scruffy around the ears. But it's the way he holds himself. Assured. Confident. Despite the fact his body is currently a taut cable, eyes red, and lips pressed in a thin line of anger.

Abby jabbers out some words, the sentences running together, hands wringing at her waist. "Baby, what are you doing here? This is nothing. It was just a study group, but then everyone left and we were drinking and hanging out and it just happened and we didn't mean to and it was an accident and it will never happen again. It means nothing."

"Nothing?" The sound of Hairy-Butt Man's zipper sliding up punctuates his word.

Silence stretches for a few seconds.

"Kevin?" Fitz says, like he's just now realized who the other person in the room is. One hand jerks in Hairy-Butt's direction. "You're fucking *Kevin*?"

"Baby—"

"Don't *baby* me." Both of Fitz's hands come up into his hair, carding through the messy strands before releasing. "We've been over for a month, and you sent me that text earlier . . . Did you *want* me to come here and find this?"

Hold on to your horses and other equine animals. They've been over for a month?

"Wait, you guys are broken up?" Kevin says, glancing from Abby to Fitz, then back to Abby again.

She's biting her lip, eyes downcast.

"Are you kidding me right now?" Fitz asks. "Is that

what you got off on, thinking you were taking someone else's girl?"

Kevin shrugs. "Seems to me she's everyone's good time. You think I'm the first one here?" Since Kevin's profile is facing me, I have a view of the corner of his mouth as it lifts in a smirk. "You think *you* were?"

I also have the perfect view to watch Fitz's thunderous expression morph into tornado territory.

There's a beat and then an explosion of movement.

Fitz tackles Kevin and they both surge in my direction—a jumble of snarled limbs tumbling onto the bed near my feet.

Shrieking, I leap away from the melee, but my feet get wrapped up in the comforter. I collapse into Abby.

She's screaming and crying and I narrowly miss one of her fists flailing toward my face.

Jerking backward, I work to untangle my arm from between Abby's legs and my heavy blanket while simultaneously trying to avoid the beatdown occurring on my bed.

She's only in a bra and panties. I've never been so close to someone so naked in my life.

I can't get away quickly enough, can't get air into my lungs. The proximity is too much. The fight is too close in the small space.

Slapping flesh and grunts from only a few feet away accompany my frantic movements. The tightness in my chest builds. I can't breathe. I can't get free. My hair snags in Abby's bra strap and the panic already choking me builds into an inferno.

One leg finally frees from the blanket and I brace it against the floor and jerk back hard, not caring about the pain in my head from losing a chunk of hair to Victoria's Secret.

Finally, something breaks loose and the momentum knocks me back. My arms windmill in the air, but I can't stop the trajectory.

I brace myself for impact, but fall short when my head smacks into something—no, *someone*. There's a loud crack and a shriek and then I'm knocked to my butt on the hard floor, the impact making my teeth rattle.

Someone is screaming, and it takes a few long seconds to realize it's not me.

It's the RA, Cynthia. She's covering her nose with a hand but it's not stopping the blood flowing freely down her face.

There's a crowd standing outside our open doorway, fellow dorm dwellers in pajamas with rumpled hair and cell phones at the ready.

I glance from Cynthia and Abby to Fitz and Kevin, who aren't fighting anymore. Fitz has Kevin's throat in one hand, his other primed for bashing, but his face is turned to the commotion. Kevin uses the distraction to push Fitz away from him. Fitz immediately shoves back but then the wailing makes them both stop. Fitz has an open cut on his lip and Kevin's eye is already swelling.

All eyes are on Cynthia holding her nose. So much blood flowing between her fingers, tap tap tapping on the hard floor.

"There are a large number of blood vessels in the

nose. It's never as bad as it looks," I say. But no one is listening.

Abby is the first to move, shrugging on a red silk robe and rushing to Cynthia.

"Did she hit you? Let me help." She shoots me a dirty look, like it's my fault, before dashing out the door, practically carrying the RA while snapping at the assembled crowd. "Somebody do something! Call someone!"

Fitz and Kevin hurry out the door after her.

Over the rush in my ears from the adrenaline and the tapping of fingers on cell phones, someone says, "Who is she?"

THE COPS IN BLUE FALLS ARE PROBABLY LIKE MOST COPS IN sleepy Texas towns: unused to exercise and overly familiar with free burgers from the Frostee Freeze on Main Street.

The last major crime in town was when someone stole three of Mr. Johnson's chickens and let them loose in the high school principal's office. That was before I went there.

The police officers don't know what to do with a bunch of sniveling coeds and the overly dramatic retellings of the "riot" that broke out in Juniper Hall on this humid autumn night.

No one is leaving, even though the officers keep asking for people to return to their rooms.

An EMT shows up and checks out Cynthia's nose.

Not broken, just bruised. They don't take her to the hospital, instead bandaging it up and giving her some painkillers.

There are only a handful of scrapes and bruises between the rest of us.

Not surprisingly, most people blame me.

"Why did she hit Cynthia?" someone in the crowd of onlookers asks.

"Does she even live here?"

I sigh, but say nothing as the cops lead Abby, Fitz, Kevin, and I downstairs to the main office on the first floor.

Once they've got us in the small room, they have us sit in hard plastic chairs facing each other, Fitz and Abby on one side, Kevin and I on the other.

The office has front-facing windows where visitors check in. It's also where dorm residents go to file complaints or talk to someone about needing light bulbs or simple repairs.

The cops stay outside the door, talking. I can't make out the words, just their lulling cadence, but no doubt they're calling the dean of students.

We sit in silence except for an occasional sniff and murmur from Abby, still trying to get Fitz to talk to her.

I'm numb and exhausted. And cold in the air-conditioned office, even with my galaxy pajama pants and bright-pink, baggy T-shirt. Despite the cold, I start nodding off, nearly falling asleep when Abby's voice escalates and yanks me awake.

"You have to forgive me," she sobs. I've never seen

her like this. Her mascara runs down her face, and her hair is a jumbled blonde mess.

She's one of those people who are always put together—like she's going to a club, not an eight a.m. class. She spends an hour each morning blow-drying her blonde hair into sleek perfection—then another hour giving herself cat eyes and pouty lips. She never leaves the room any other way. It's surprising to see her a wreck.

"I don't have to do anything." Fitz's jaw is clenched, his arms crossed over his chest. He leans as far away from Abby as he can get in the cramped space.

I have so many questions. Fitz said they were over. I didn't imagine it. But Abby never let on anything about them breaking up. If anything, her boasting about Fitz being in her pocket has increased over the last month. Why did they break up? And if they did, why did he show up here tonight and defend her when Kevin spewed his vitriol?

"What are you staring at?" Fitz is glaring at me now, the acerbic and unexpected attention making my cheeks heat and my heart race. "Why are you here anyway? What were you doing in there? Watching the show?"

My mouth pops open but no sound emerges. His eyes flash with anger and it's directed at me and I don't know how to respond. People don't talk to me unless it's a quick "excuse me" or "sorry" when we collide, because I'm tiny and forgettable. There's nothing special about my plain brown hair and plain blue eyes and plain features.

I'm not used to confrontation, not since my first week

at Blue Falls High four years ago, before I learned how to be invisible.

For sure, no one has ever antagonized me about daring to try and sleep in my own room during a brawl I neither asked for nor instigated.

I mean, imagine my audacity, trying to sleep in my own bed on a Monday night.

All of these thoughts fly through my head at Mach three, followed by an imagined scenario where I'm telling him he's a Neanderthal prick with a girlfriend who has more insecurities than China has people.

But I'm frozen. An iceberg. The *Titanic* could hit me and still, I'd remain. My mouth pops open but no sound emerges.

Surprisingly, Abby comes to my rescue. "She's my roommate."

They're all staring at me now. And still, I can't speak. Just a block of ice.

"She deaf?" Kevin drawls.

"Leave her alone," Abby snaps and for a second, warmth kindles in my chest. Is someone actually standing up for me? Abby? Of all people?

But then she continues speaking. "She's got special needs."

The heat in my chest fizzles and dies. "I don't have . . ." The words are a broken ignition on my lips, not quite catching. No time to speak, anyway.

The door opens. The dean of students is here in his flannel pajamas, his hair rumpled and his eyes angry.

"I can explain everything," Abby says, her lashes wet with unshed tears.

The dean's expression doesn't lighten at her pleading tone. If anything, it darkens as he stomps into the room.

2

No person is your friend who demands your silence, or denies your right to grow.
—Alice Walker

Fitz

"You boys have somewhere else to be or you want to stay and get citations?" The dean glares at both Kevin and I hard enough to jolt us out of our chairs, scrambling for the exit.

He's letting us go.

We're lucky. I doubt Abby and . . . whoever the other person is will be as fortunate.

Once outside the office, the door slams behind us and I stall out, unresolved emotions lingering in my gut.

I want to run as far away from Abby as possible, and yet I'm also not done venting my frustration on someone.

Anyone.

The cops are gone, the lower floor of the dorms empty and dim. I pull out my phone. It's four o'clock in the morning.

"Do you need a ride home?" Kevin asks.

We live in the same house. I'm going to have to stare at his stupid smug face for the rest of the semester. There's gotta be a way to avoid him.

The booming voice of the dean echoes from inside the office.

Something about "orders of removal" and "appeal rights."

I don't bother answering Kevin, instead walking away.

He runs to catch up, following me through the front doors and out into the dark parking lot. "Why did you and Abby break up?"

"It's none of your business."

"Why didn't you tell me it was over?"

I shake my head and keep walking.

"You know, she's still telling everyone you're together."

I shouldn't engage, but I'm still too worked up to remain silent. "And that's why you thought it was a good idea to hook up with her? Because you thought you were getting one over on me?" I stop long enough to laugh in his face. "You're pathetic."

Almost to my truck now.

"No more pathetic than you fighting over a girl who isn't even yours."

I don't argue with that, but Kevin doesn't understand. She might not be mine in the sense he means, but Abby and I have been friends since we were barely out of diapers. Sticking up for her is like second nature. No matter our past history, I could never stand idly by while someone hurt her. Even though doing so may have made things worse, for her and definitely for me.

I don't think I can stare at Kevin's smug face any longer without punching him again, and I still have to live with the guy.

Hopping into my beaten old Ford pickup, I slam the door. I half expect Kevin to continue our argument despite the door between us. He loves a good row, but instead, he smirks at me through the window before jogging back into the building.

Great. He can be her knight in shining armor.

That's not me. Not anymore. This is exactly why I broke it off with Abby in the first place. We are too different.

Besides the gulf that's slowly grown over the last year, I'm almost eighty percent certain she started cheating on me right after we started college. She's changed too much and I can't handle the drama.

When I finally broke it off, she was surprisingly calm and understanding. But then the random texts and phone calls started, and I kept responding to them like a fool, and now it's all culminated in this.

I take stock of my sore knuckles and swollen lip. I guess it could be worse.

Earlier, in the middle of the night, Abby woke me with a text.

I wish I could go to sleep and not wake up.

Immediately I tried to call her, but she didn't answer. I tried a few times more, then tried to go back to sleep, but I couldn't.

I was worried. Now . . . I don't know what to think.

The drive home is quick. Scott's parents have a rental property right off campus so I'm walking in the door within minutes.

I grab a bag of frozen green beans and head to my room, right down the hall from Kevin's. I grimace at his shut door. It's going to be even more hellish to live with him now.

It's not that I'm jealous. I'm not. I don't want to be with Abby anymore, but it still hurts. We were a couple for so long and friends for even longer. It's like she wanted me to see her with Kevin. She wanted to try and make me angry or jealous, or who knows. I still hear the sound when I close my eyes.

Thump. Thump. Thump.

My stomach rolls, remembering what Kevin said. *You think I'm the first one here? You think* you *were?*

I doze in and out, never quite reaching dreamland since my hand throbs from where I punched Kevin in his stupid face.

The sound of someone talking pulls me from my half

sleep. I'm still fully dressed, eyes gritty. I look over at my alarm. It's one o'clock.

I've missed all my classes today.

I need coffee. I head to the kitchen and start the pot, grabbing a cup from the worn-out cupboard and straining to hear Scott talking.

He's on the phone, his voice low. I can't make out much, but Kevin's name comes up. And mine.

Once the coffee is done brewing, Scott's voice has gone silent. I head out to the porch and sit on the rickety old folding chair.

He's leaning against the railing, eyes inscrutable. "We need to talk."

My heart thumps, a dull pulsing in my head, which is starting to throb along with my hand. "About what?" I blow on the coffee before taking a sip.

"There's no easy way to say this."

No way. He got to Scott already. It's only been . . . well, it's nearly one, so I guess it's been about eight hours.

"I don't think it's a good idea if you keep staying here."

Before I can figure out how to respond, a car pulls into the driveway.

Abby's Mini Cooper.

She got it for her eighteenth birthday. I helped her dad pick it out. It's black with red racing stripes, and Abby cried happy tears when her dad handed her the keys. Then we drove it to the Frostee Freeze for ice cream cones and went parking at the lake.

I put the coffee cup down on the porch next to the

chair, but I can't set aside a lifetime of memories with the same ease. I face Scott. "What is going on?"

"Sorry, Fitz." At least he has the grace to look as uncomfortable as I feel. He won't meet my eyes.

"Why are you giving me the boot?"

He blinks at me, his hands flexing against the straps of his bag on his shoulders. "You punched Kevin."

"He deserved it."

Scott winces, rubbing the back of his neck with a hand. "Maybe. But I can't kick him out. He pays rent."

"I can pay rent."

He lets me stay here for free. It's why I moved in. I actually can't afford to pay rent, but I also can't afford to be homeless. I could work something out. Get a job. I push away thoughts of how that might affect my grades, my cross-country scholarship . . .

I can make it work. I have to.

"Kev is my best friend. One of you has to go, and I can't kick him out. Besides, you probably won't want to stay here anyway since Abby's moving in. She was kicked out of the dorms." Scott shuffles his feet and glances over at Abby's car, where Kevin is hauling a bag out of the trunk.

I lean forward, elbows on my knees, head in my hands. I understand Scott is in a bind. He hates confrontation and this conversation is probably killing him. But I'm tired and I can't deal with this. I've already missed classes today and I've got to keep my grades up.

"So that's it, huh?"

"You have somewhere to go. Your parents live nearby,

right?"

Maybe. It will be weird. Dad's off work on injury and they're both stressed to the max. They don't need my problems or another mouth to feed.

But maybe it's the best option, even though I haven't told them yet Abby and I are over. We had decided to hold off informing our parents until we had to.

Now I'll have no choice.

Feet thump on the steps and stalls our conversation. Not that there's anything else to say.

"I'm sorry, Fitz. Really, I am."

I stand up, but Scott leaves then, passing Kevin and Abby on the stairs with a couple quick words.

Kevin passes into the house after a smirk in my direction. I manage to hold back any response, although I do feel a bit of satisfaction at the darkening bruises around his eye.

Then Abby is there, standing at the top of the porch, eyes still rimmed in red, reminding me of when we were thirteen and Tommy Phillips called her a bitch. My hand throbbed that day too.

"Can I talk to you?" Her voice wavers.

My whole body is tense, but I can't help the pang of something resembling sympathy underneath. Despite everything that's happened between us over the last year, a lifetime of memories is not something I can discard easily. This is so confusing. Too many conflicting emotions. Anger. Pain. But I still care. I wish I didn't.

Then I might not be in this situation.

"I'm sorr—"

"Don't say it." I swipe the words away with a hand. "I'm not ready to hear you apologize."

"I know you hate me. You have every right. But Fitz, please . . ." She breaks away, her gaze falling to her hands wringing in front of her. "Please don't tell our parents yet."

Any sympathy I have evaporates.

That's what she's worried about? Not about me or my feelings or where I'm going to live now? The fact that she's been acting crazy and manipulating me for the last month? Longer, actually. I didn't see the full picture until now.

"I have to tell my parents. I have nowhere else to live, Abby. They're gonna wonder why I can't stay here anymore." It was the luckiest of breaks, or so I thought. I wouldn't be here if it weren't for the scholarship and Scott's offer of a free room.

I have to tell my parents, and they'll tell Abby's parents. After all, our mommas have been best friends since we were kids. She doesn't want her parents to find out so she doesn't have to deal with them. What an inconvenience for her.

"Please, Fitz. The truth is, I'm already in a spot of trouble. And it's bad." She bites her lip in a move that used to elicit sympathy and arousal, but now only makes me sick. She continues, "My grades aren't great. If I can't bring them up, I might have to drop out."

I rock back on my heels. "What? Since when?"

But she doesn't answer my question. "If my parents find out I got kicked out of the dorms on top of everything else . . ." She shakes her head. "I need you to do this one thing for me. It's not forever. I can appeal the decision and maybe move back into the dorms, but it takes a couple months."

"Why didn't you tell me about your grades?"

She swallows and tears stream down her face. "Because it's embarrassing enough. I'll deal with everything, but it would help if my parents didn't know. You know how Daddy is."

Her dad is a perfectionist and expects the same from his daughter. Always has. And Abby has always lived up to those expectations, until now.

"Where am I supposed to live for two months, Abby? In my truck?"

"I'm sure you'll find something. There's Annabel too."

My sister. I guess it's possible I could stay with her temporarily, but she has roommates. The housing situation in Blue Falls right now is a nightmare.

I clench my jaw, wishing for a miracle, to go back in time, and for everything in the last twelve hours to not have happened. I can't possibly let her do this. But then I meet Abby's blue eyes, as familiar as my own, now red with tears. Her face is pale, her arms wrapped around her stomach like it's the only thing holding her together. The angry ball in my stomach turns hollow.

"Fine."

She disappears inside and I stay on the porch for a minute, wondering how on earth everything could have gone so wrong so quickly.

I get all my stuff in the truck in less than a half hour without running into Abby or Kevin. They've disappeared into his room, the door shut. All is quiet.

I don't have much, but it's enough to almost fill the two-seater cab of my truck. I won't be able to sleep here, unless I do so while sitting up with a box for a pillow.

I sit in the driveway in my now-cramped cab and call the only person who might be able to help me find a place to live, even though it's the last person I want to call because of the sheer amount of shit she's going to give me.

Annabel.

I take a deep breath before hitting the call button. Gotta pull it together. Time to get things sorted.

"Hey, Annabel Lee. How's your tomb in the sounding sea?" I shouldn't be teasing her since I'm about to ask a favor, but it's an old joke.

"You're not at all worth pleasing, Mr. Darcy," she counters.

Our mother is a librarian. She loves all things literature, hence our names.

Dad—who doesn't read anything except construction plans—might have argued, but he loved her too much to tell her no. Our parents have been together since they were children. Just like Abby and I.

My stomach lurches but I pull it together and remind myself of the conversation at hand.

"So how you been?" I ask.

There's a long second of silence and then Annabel responds in a wary tone. "What do you want, Fitz?"

I sigh. Better to get it over with. "Can I crash on your couch for a few days?"

A longer stretch of silence ensues. "What's going on?"

"There's been a bit of an issue here."

"Aren't you staying at Scott's?"

"It's a long story."

She pauses. "Please don't tell me your psycho girlfriend has something to do with this."

"Okay, I won't tell you."

"Fitz!"

"What? And she's not a psycho." Also, she's no longer my girlfriend. Also, the psycho thing might be more accurate than I've wanted to believe but the natural urge to defend Abby is going to be a hard one to break.

"I'm not convinced."

Even though Abby isn't my favorite person at the moment, I don't really want to tell Annabel the entire horror story. But I'm not seeing any way around it at the moment. If she feels bad enough for me, I won't have to beg too much for a spot on her couch. "Don't be all gleeful about this, Annabel, you hear me?"

She sighs. "I'm not happy if you're in pain, blah blah blah, now tell me what's going on so I can come up with a solution."

I take a breath before letting it out. Quick. Like a Band-Aid. "Abby and I broke up."

"What?" Her shriek could wake the entire county. "When?"

"About a month ago."

"A month? A month! What the hell, Fitz?"

"I don't wanna get into the details. It's over. But we were still friends, then she . . . she was sending me weird texts last night and I got worried and went to check on her and I caught her and Kevin. In her dorm. On the floor."

She hisses and I can practically feel her breathing fire through the line. "Your roommate Kevin? She was banging your roommate? Did you kill them? Because if you haven't, I want a shot at it."

"I might have hit Kevin. A few times."

"You should have punched Abby. She's the one who likes to set up the dominos just to tap one with her overly manicured finger and watch them fall. Right onto people's heads."

"I don't want to talk about it. I know you've never liked her."

"That's not true, I liked her fine until she started wearing pants so tight you could see her religion."

A startled laugh escapes me. "I don't know what you mean."

"Come on, Fitz. She hasn't been the same since you guys went off to college together. I could tell last summer at the midnight hay ride she was looking to park her car in someone else's garage."

She's right. It's why I ended things already, and yet I still got sucked into her crap. I thump my head against the steering wheel. I have been blind. "I get it and you're right, okay? You're always right. Are you happy now?"

"Kind of. I would like to hear it again in person. Maybe in writing too."

"I have a more pressing problem. I have nowhere to live."

"You could go home. I mean, I know it will be strange and all since Dad's not working but you still have a room there."

How can I tell her? "I can't tell Momma."

"Oh my God. Don't tell me Abby is making you keep this a secret? Because she's so selfish, it's all about her."

"I didn't say that."

"You don't have to." She groans in frustration. "I get it, Fitz. I know you think you should have some kind of Lifetime-movie love story like our parents, but sometimes life isn't like that. You've got a skewed vision of reality."

But that's the thing. Abby and I did have an epic love story. Just like my parents and my grandparents. "Why are you such a cynic? Wait. Don't answer." I've gone down this road with Annabel before. She thinks love is all a "social construct," despite the fact that our own parents have been together for almost thirty years and are still as in love as the day they first met. "I didn't call to argue with you. I need a place to crash for a little bit."

Annabel is like a prickly pear—a tough exterior hiding a soft center.

She's quiet for a few seconds before speaking. "I'm sorry, Fitz, but you can't stay at my place."

"Why not?"

"We've got three women in a two-bedroom condo. Susie and Christie just got married. It's not happening."

She lives with a couple she met in journalism school.

They've all been roommates since her last year of college.

"I'll sleep in the bathtub. I'm desperate."

"One, it's a stand-up shower. Two, they're newlyweds and want to be alone. I promised them I would start looking for a new place myself. I'm lucky they're cutting me some slack since the market is so bad right now."

A local landowner found a cave full of blue topaz last year, bringing a ton of mining and business to an area just outside our sleepy little town, but also sucking up all available housing. They've started building new apartments to fill the gap, but it hasn't caught up to the demand. It's a nightmare to find anywhere to live.

"So, then what are my other options?"

"If you can't stay at home and you can't stay with me . . . maybe try the housing center on campus?"

"You really think there's going to be something? It's a month into the semester."

"You never know," Annabel says. "You might get lucky. Or grow a set of balls, tell everyone the truth, and let Abby go to hell."

"I guess I could give Dad a heart attack as well as a bad back."

My guilt trip doesn't work. Annabel just sighs. "Let me know what you decide. And . . . hey, I'll keep an eye on the ads at the paper. Maybe someone somewhere is renting a room. I'll get you first look."

"Thanks, sis."

We hang up and I rub at my tired eyes.

Guess I'm heading to the housing center.

3

A wise woman wishes to be no one's enemy; a wise woman refuses to be anyone's victim.
—Maya Angelou

Reese

Scarlett's phone goes straight to voice mail.

"Hey. It's me. Your sister." Why did I say that? She knows who I am. Ugh, I can't escape the awkward even with family. "I know you're busy, but . . . can you call me? Whenever you can. Miss you."

I end the call and slump back in the drivers' seat.

My eyes are dry and grubby. I still can't believe it. I've been kicked out of the dorms, of any official university housing. I can appeal the decision, but it has to go in front of the housing board and not for another month, at least. I can request an emergency session but that involves paperwork and waiting and a bunch of bureaucratic malarkey that will probably get me nowhere since I have family locally.

Tears burn behind my eyes but I refuse to let them fall.

Scarlett would tell me to find the bright side. She's the only person who really understands me. But she moved to New York last year and now she's starting some kind of food truck so she can pay her big-city rent and she's too busy to deal with my problems.

I take a deep breath and try and look at the positive aspects of my current situation.

It's the basis of cognitive behavioral therapy—imitating optimism and the things you want in your life to help you actualize them.

I take a deep breath. Okay. Here we go. Bright side. I didn't want to live with Abby anyway. Going home is better. More comfortable. I'll actually get some sleep. I won't be derided constantly. I won't have to see people so much. People don't generally like me and I've never gotten close enough to determine if I like them either.

I'll have more time to myself. I won't be expected to socialize. I won't be judged for my lack of fancy clothes, my affinity for books, or the way I talk.

The only thing I'll have to deal with at home is Granny.

The thought makes me wince.

She might be more trouble than it's worth.

I pull out of the dorm parking lot and into traffic, glancing back to watch the building disappear in my rear view.

The first day I moved into the dorms, Abby took one look at my plain T-shirt and simple haircut and rolled her eyes. Then she saw my advanced class schedule and things really went downhill.

I was never cool enough. Pretty enough. Social enough. Never *enough* enough to be friends with her and her clique. Or anyone really.

I throw away the memories of the past year living with Abby and the hell that came with it. I have more important issues to contend with.

I pass through Main Street and head north, past the Frostee Freeze, where the popular kids gather for burgers and ice cream, past the movie theater that only has two showings on weekends, all places I don't go.

I wave at ol' Roy, a local homeless man who sits outside the H-E-B and waves at everyone who drives by. Well, almost everyone.

He doesn't see me.

He never does.

Sigh.

I pass the sign at the city limits. *Now leaving Blue Falls. Y'all come back now, ya hear!* The blue cartoon boar painted on the corner is forever frozen with an eternal smile, waving one hoof in the air.

Five minutes later, I'm navigating down the wide gravel drive toward home.

Granny is on the porch, sitting in a bright-yellow

chair, her red overalls clashing with the navy blue of the large barn-style front door. The giant ranch house is painted in a variety of eclectic colors—orange shutters, red trim, blue shingles—and yet it somehow works in a weird, artsy, avant-garde way. Just like my parents, colorful and weird.

It's good to be home. Except . . . Granny's holding a shotgun.

Not necessarily an unusual sight.

I get out and pop the trunk, grabbing my backpack. "Are you shooting rabbits in the front yard again?" I call out when I'm nearly to the porch steps.

She loves to Elmer Fudd her way around the front yard, chasing those wiley wabbits and yelling about how they eat her lettuce and turnips and poop all over her grass. "Nope. Got a call from the university today."

Well, crap on Copernicus. "I can explain—"

"You get right back in that car and go on back to school, you hear?" She stands up, still holding the gun.

"But I have nowhere to live. I got . . . they kicked me out of the dorms. There's nowhere else for me to stay."

She's shaking her head before I even finish my story or have a chance to explain fully. "You can't stay here, Tootsie Roll. You need to find your own way. It's like I always say, life is like a box of condoms. You need to use them for good living or protection. But . . . you know, the terms aren't mutually exclusive."

"What?" That doesn't make sense. Not that anything Granny says ever really makes sense. She's always mixing up her expressions and making up random ones.

"It's for your own good, okay? Oh, and take the bag of clothes there with you." She motions with the gun to a brown paper grocery bag. "It's about time you got back. I love you and I'll see you on Sunday for dinner. Get on back now." She makes a shooing gesture with the gun.

I pick up the bag, recognizing the bright shirt folded neatly on top—one I bought on a shopping trip with Scarlett before I started high school, years ago.

"You're not going to shoot me."

She cocks the gun, but keeps it pointed at the deck. "You sure about that?"

I'm not.

Maybe she won't shoot to kill, but to frighten and potentially maim? Wouldn't put it past her.

Everyone in my family has been pushing me to socialize and make friends and "get out there." Well, now I've been out there. I know Granny thinks this is some kind of tough love gesture, but right now it's more tough than love.

We stare at each other, a game of chicken I've played with Granny before, but never when she had a shotgun in her hand.

And I've never won.

Therefore, it's not surprising when I blink first.

"I wish I had a normal family!" I yell over my shoulder while setting my backpack and now an extra bag of clothes in the trunk.

"Wish in one hand, shit in the other," Granny calls back. "You tell me which hand gets filled first."

And this is how I become homeless. Will I have to

sleep in my car? It's a 1967 two-door Volkswagen Beetle. Not exactly livable space.

Maybe I should call Scarlett again. Tell her what's going on. She could talk sense into Granny. Maybe.

But beyond that, I can't ask for anything. She can't send me money she doesn't have to spare, and even if she could, where would I go? The roach motel on the south edge of town? Even that is likely full at the moment.

I take a deep breath. I can do this. I'm going to solve this problem on my own. I'm an adult. Nineteen years old.

The lump in my throat expands, despite the pep talk.

I guess I'll try the housing center first.

THANKFULLY, THE OFFICE ISN'T TOO BUSY. PROBABLY because it's a month into the semester and everyone has a place to live by now.

The two clerks have students in front of them, but there's no line. I stand behind the yellow tape and wait my turn.

The door opens behind me, letting in a too-warm breeze despite the fact that it's nearly October, and I turn my head.

It's him.

Fitz.

Abby's boyfriend. Or ex-boyfriend, I reckon.

He's in the same clothes from early this morning,

except he's added a ball cap tugged down low over his eyes.

We lock gazes and as soon as the flash of recognition hits his face, I flip around like a rabbit running from a snake.

My face burns. Smoldering. Combusting.

I still can't believe he thought I was watching Abby and her faux beau do it on the floor. Like I ever wanted any part of it. The way he looked at me . . . like I was some kind of freak.

She's got special needs.

I shake the thought away and tug at my shorts. Glancing down, I notice a dark ink stain right near the crotch, next to a greyish brown dirt smudge, probably from moving boxes. Ugh.

I straighten my spine and focus on the clerks behind the counter, remembering that Fitz doesn't matter. What he thinks of me is irrelevant. He's probably just like Abby, who delighted in making comments like, *I love how you don't care what people think,* and *Is that really the look you're going for?* or *You look pretty in your own way, I suppose.* Insults sometimes disguised as compliments and sometimes not, meant to make me feel as small as possible.

Did it make her feel bigger?

One of the students at the counter steps away and I shrug off my thoughts. It's all over now. With any luck, I'll never see Abby Summers again.

The clerk calls me up and I set my bag on the

counter, knocking over her pen cup and watching in horror as writing utensils and paper clips spill out and tumble to the floor in a loud, jangling clutter.

My face, already enflamed, heats even further while I bend over to pick up the items, apologizing at least three times before saying in a breathless rush, "I'm so sorry but I need a home. I mean, I have a home but I can't go back there because I might get shot."

The clerk stares at me, wide-eyed.

And this is why I don't talk to folks I don't know. It's like my brain jams up and the words get muddled and hazy or pop outta my mouth like Mexican jumping beans.

"I mean . . ." I take a deep breath and focus. "I'm looking for housing. Is there anywhere for rent?"

In my periphery, Fitz steps up to the other clerk. He says something, much more coherently than I managed, I'm sure, but I keep my gaze focused on the brunette in front of me and try not to listen.

Then the two workers speak at once. "Check the bulletin board."

My ears prick. It's like surround sound in here.

Fitz's eyes lock on mine, tangled together for a hot second. Then we're in motion, speed walking to the board in the corner. It's mostly empty—save for the Blue Falls Fighting Boars sticker up in one corner and there, in the center, a lone piece of paper.

Although we reach it at the same time, he's faster and lengthier. His hand snatches the sheet and then he's walking away without another word, long legs carrying him out the door.

I gape after him.

I can't believe it. He's the reason I'm homeless to begin with. If he hadn't come barging into my room, starting a brawl with his erstwhile girlfriend and her paramour, this wouldn't have happened.

The past twenty-four hours have been a nightmare of which I had no control and he . . . now he . . .

My heart is racing in my chest, pumping my veins with something I'm not used to. My breathing increases.

I'm angry.

No. I'm so mad I could spit.

This isn't fair. None of it is my fault. I let it slide when Abby partied in our room at all hours. I didn't complain when she made snide remarks about my clothes, my books, my everything.

All my life I've let other people dictate what I do. I didn't even really want to go to college. I could have learned just as much on my own. But my parents made me and I acquiesced, because that's what I do.

Then Scarlett moved out and she's the one who convinced me to live in the dorms. Told me I needed to learn how to adapt, since high school was such a bust. It would be different, she said. People change as they get older.

My own Granny won't even let me go home. And now this . . . this *guy*, is going to take away the only opportunity I have left? Like I don't matter?

There's a roaring in my ears, a giant wave crashing all around me.

I won't be shoved around. I can't be invisible. Not anymore. Even if it means embarrassment and shame and acting a fool. I've already gone through all that for the last five years and look where that got me.

Slamming against the door with more force than intended—which is a terrible idea because it takes me a full five seconds to realize it's *pull* and not *push*—I eventually make it through and down the sidewalk after Fitz.

My heart thumps in time with my feet slapping the pavement as I race to keep up with his loping stride. It's afternoon and there aren't many students walking around so I don't have any problems spotting Fitz's lanky form up ahead on the sidewalk.

He stops suddenly and turns to face me, shrugging his backpack up further on his shoulders.

"Why are you following me?" he asks, voice rough.

I'm worse than a deer in headlights. I'm a mole. A muskrat. A bat that's lived in a cave alone for so long it can't comprehend the screech of fellow mammals. I mentally pry my tongue from the roof of my mouth and clench my anger like a weapon.

"You can't take the whole flyer," I manage without sounding like a loon. Progress. Maybe if I keep the sentences short and to the point, then my brain won't get off track.

"Looks like that's what I did." He turns and keeps walking.

I continue to trail behind him.

"Stop following me," he calls over his shoulder, speeding up even more.

"Maybe there will be more than one room."

"If there isn't, I'm getting it."

"But I need a place to live."

He turns down the next street, legs eating up the sidewalk. "So do I."

"I have nowhere else." I push the words out in between panting breaths. I'm running to keep up with his stride. A bead of sweat rolls down my back.

"Me neither."

"I'm a girl!"

He stops to face me. "That's sexist."

He's right. I shouldn't have played that card. Also, I'm not really a *girl*, am I? I'm a woman. My face heats.

Darn it all to Hamlet.

At my silence, he heads up the sidewalk toward a one-story brick house.

This must be the place. It looks like the kind of house a little old lady would live in. Not an old lady like my granny, who makes moonshine and threatens her granddaughter with death and dismemberment, but one who makes cherry pie every day and has a million cats and calls everyone "sweetie."

There are clean white shutters and a bay window, which from the outside looks like it could be the perfect reading nook.

The place is well maintained, with its neatly mown grass and perfectly trimmed hedges. It all fits the little-old-lady theory except for the two garden gnomes placed in a compromising position in the flower bed. Oh, and the keg on the porch.

I scramble after Fitz, who's already knocking on the door. The concrete patio is narrow and I push for a place in front of the door next to him.

Our arms brush and I catch a whiff of his cologne, which is actually quite nice smelling even though he looks like hell warmed over and has an attitude lower than a snake's belly in a wagon rut.

The door swings open. It's a scruffy man in a bathrobe. Except it's not like any robe I've ever seen. It's fancy—a velvety material covered in . . . are those cats?

He's also holding a sleepy white cat that perfectly matches the felines on his robe.

He is definitely not the little old lady of my imagination, with his longish brown hair and scruffy beard. He vaguely resembles Jesus, actually, the one depicted in the Baptist church Granny goes to, with pale skin and blue eyes.

An old-fashioned wooden pipe sticks out the corner of his mouth, all curved with an ornate stem.

He grins at us around the lip of the pipe, and then out of the bowl blows a stream of bubbles.

Jesus never blew bubbles, at least not in my Sunday school.

"What do we have here?" he asks.

"You have a room for rent?" Fitz holds up the flyer.

Bubble man eyes the flyer, glances down at me, then returns his gaze to Fitz. He pulls the pipe from his mouth and waves it around with his free hand. "You both want it? I charge extra for double tenancy."

"Do you have more than one room?" I ask.

"Nope. Just the one. One twin bed." He grins at me.

Heat creeps up my face. What is he suggesting?

At this rate I will be permanently tainted red by the end of the day.

"I'll take it," Fitz says quickly.

I speak past my dry mouth. "No, I'll take it." I try to step in front of him and Fitz blocks me with one giant foot.

"Babies." The Jesus look-alike lifts his hands. "Please. No bickering on the porch." He steps back, opening the door further. "Why don't y'all come in?"

I follow Fitz into the entryway and then we both follow bubble man into the living room.

After meeting Hugh Hefner in a cat-covered robe, I sort of expected the interior to be a mess. A bachelor pad. Maybe some street signs on the walls, stained carpets, and patio furniture in the living room. But it's surprisingly homey. The couch is faded, a loveseat covered in brown roses that may have been red at one point, but otherwise in good shape. The rest of the furniture is comfortable, the wooden floors are clean, and the rugs are simple, a deep, solid red, but nice. More like my imaginary cat lady than crazy college guy. Although he's older than your average frat boy. Maybe midtwenties. Bubbles notwithstanding.

He sits in a leather recliner and gestures for us to

take a seat on the couch with his pipe. "My name's Jude Parker. But you probably already knew that."

Fitz speaks. "Actually, I didn't—"

"Before we get into why you both want to live here, I should inform you of the ground rules to make sure it won't change your mind. This is a party house." His eyes land on me. "My business runs on social gatherings. If you complain about noise, you're out. If you bring unnecessary drama or fighting into my place of residence, you're out. If you don't clean up after yourself, you're out. If you don't put out, you're out."

"What?" My jaw drops.

"I'm okay with all of that," Fitz says.

I gape at him.

Jude puts up his hands. "It was a joke! Neither of you are my type." He pauses to set the cat on the ground. The white furball rolls over and stretches out its paws in a sleepy yawn. "And I hope neither of you are allergic to cats because Mr. Bojangles ain't going nowhere."

"We don't want to share a room," Fitz says. "You have to pick one of us." He glances over at me and then back at Jude. "And I would like to point out I was here first."

"We were here at the same time. I need a place to stay too. And it's his fault I'm homeless." I jerk my thumb at Fitz.

"It is not my fault—" he starts.

"It is *so* your—"

"Listen. Babies." Jude winces and rubs his head. "You can both sleep in the bed together. It will be tight quarters but as long as there's no drama—"

"No!" Our voices tangle in the air, his indignant, mine disgusted.

"You have to choose one of us," Fitz says.

"I can cook," I say.

Fitz glares at me. "I give killer back rubs."

"I give killer foot rubs."

"You can't copy me."

"I just did."

Jude frowns at us. "This is too much tension. I'll find someone else for the room. Y'all can see yourselves out." He waves a dismissive hand in our general direction.

"Well, hold on now," Fitz says. "I'm sure we can come to some kind of arrangement."

"I'm not so sure about that." Jude taps a finger on the arm of the chair and regards us with sharp eyes. "I can only give one of you the room, and you both seem to want it real bad." He leans his head back with a sigh and sticks the pipe in his mouth, blowing out some more bubbles. Mr. Bojangles swipes at one with a lazy paw.

"Wait." The pipe leaves his mouth. "Beast!" I jump at the shout.

A large man emerges from the hallway. He has dark hair and shoulders so broad he has to turn sideways through the arched doorway into the living room. Where did he come from? He stands there staring at us with his broad face and nearly black eyes. He has to be nearly seven feet tall and wide as a firehouse.

"Write this down," Jude tells him. "These two are fighting for the right to live in my kingdom. It's a battle . . . to the death!"

Fitz and I exchange a startled glance.

"I'm not fighting a girl," Fitz says.

I cross my arms and throw his earlier words back at him. "That's sexist."

Jude groans. "This ain't the *Hunger Games*, you boob. You won't really be fighting to the death. That was for dramatic effect. We'll keep it safe and legal. Well, except for the betting part, but no one ever gives no never mind about that. It's gonna be a test of wills. A battle of the minds. Various challenges set up by yours truly. And Beast, we can take bets on who will win each competition. The rest of the babies will love this." His eyes are gleaming as he rubs his bearded chin in thought. "I can come up with something extra special for Begonia Day. Are you writing this down?"

Sure enough, the giant that is Beast has a notebook in his hands, a normal eight by eleven spiral, but in his hands, it looks like it was made for a doll.

"This is genius," Jude continues. "I'm going to make so much money."

"Wait." Fitz glances over at Beast and then back at Jude. "That's all well and good for you, but I'm not sure I want to engage in any kind of illegal activity."

"You won't be doing anything of the sort. I will. And if you don't like it, the door's over yonder." He gestures in the direction we came in with his pipe.

There's a tense silence during which I hold my breath and hope Fitz decides to get up and leave.

But no such luck.

Instead, he sits back and crosses his arms over his

chest. "Where would we sleep in the meantime? While all this . . . competition is going on?"

Jude sits back in the recliner with his hands behind his head, crossing his feet. Mr. Bojangles jumps up into his lap and settles. "You can take turns. One in the room, one out here on the couch." He gestures to the rose-patterned sofa. "It's not good. Kinda small. There's some lumps. Plus people are always here late at night so you might not actually sleep much." His eyes brighten with an idea. "Whoever wins the game of the day can get the room until the next competition. A little added incentive."

I glance around the living room. This sounds like a terrible idea. A party house? Me? People? All the time?

But then Jude continues, "And if you both agree, I won't even charge rent until the whole competition is over." He grins around the pipe. "I'll make so much money off you two, I won't even need it. One week. Two challengers. Seven games. Endless possibilities." His eyes are gleaming.

Beast clears his throat with a loud rumble and Jude nods, like he can interpret the sound.

"Right, right." He tilts his head. "Two weeks. Every other day. I'll need time to plan and execute each challenge."

My mind, reeling from this whole conversation, picks up his words and thinks them through. "So . . . if I win the first four games, will the room be mine?" I ask slowly.

"Nope."

"That doesn't make sense," Fitz says.

“My house, my rules.” His brows lift. “You don’t like it? There are at least twenty other people who would die to live here.”

Fitz answers for us. “No, no, it’s fine.”

Jude’s hands clap together, startling me. “Great. We begin tonight.”

4

I've never been one to run from a challenge.
—Patrick Swayze

Fitz

"Kitchen." Jude flourishes one arm, like we're on a TV show about fancy multimillion-dollar cribs instead of a small kitchen with ancient cabinets and worn linoleum. "We take turns cooking supper. Rotation is on the fridge." He points to a white board calendar. "Nothing too fancy. Beast makes a mean jambalaya. Hope you like it hot. For all your other meals and snacks, buy and label your own. Ask before borrowing items that don't belong to you. Kindergarten rules apply. Questions?"

"No," I answer.

Reese says nothing, just gives a quick shake of her head.

Before the tour, Jude had us sign liability waivers, documents he procured from a drawer in the living room. I peeked at hers while we were filling them out. It was the only way I could figure out her name, since she hasn't uttered a peep since we agreed to this whole thing, let alone taken the time to introduce herself.

It should be concerning Jude had such a thing on hand for us to sign, but I can't find it in me to question or complain. At least I'm not sleeping in my truck tonight.

We follow Jude out the kitchen and down the hall toward the back of the house. "Here's the bathroom." He pushes open a door and flicks on the light. "Beast and I share the one at the back of the house. The one for public consumption is off to the side of the dining room, next to the laundering area. Y'all get this one, but people will probably still use it when it gets busy around here. Keep it clean, babies."

One small sink, more warped linoleum. An old white claw-foot tub with a low showerhead.

Across the hall, he opens another door. "And here it is. The room you've all been waiting for." He flicks the switch and Christmas lights come on, strung around the top of the room.

I stick a head in the door and peer around. "But it's October."

Jude shrugs. "Ran out of lamps."

He wasn't kidding about the room being tiny. There's a narrow bed shoved in one corner, a three-drawer dresser that would be insufficient for a toddler, and a closet that doesn't even span the length of my forearm. It's all topped off with a murky smell of dust and disuse. Like it was recently a storage closet before being converted.

And somehow, we have to cram all of our crap in here while we compete for the "opportunity" to live here indefinitely.

"I've got only one key. I recommend keeping the room locked up at night when things get social. Whoever wins the challenge will get to be guardian of the key till the next challenge, but you can keep it unlocked during the day for general use and access to personal belongings. The rest of the babies—the ones who don't live here—aren't allowed in until after five every day, so your items will be secure."

"Storage?" I ask.

He nods toward the closet.

"Right."

So basically, I'll be keeping everything but clothes and necessities stuffed in the cab of my truck. Great.

"I'll leave you two to get settled in. We'll be meeting in the backyard after supper—access available via the slider in the living room or the door through the garage. It's Beast's night for cooking and I'll take care of it tomorrow night to give y'all a chance to get used to the routine."

"Mighty kind of you." The words come out a bit more sarcastic than I intended, but it doesn't seem to faze Jude.

He gives us a lazy smile. "I aim to please. Later, babies."

He disappears down the hall.

I turn toward Reese, but she's already gone, walking down the hall toward the front door without a word.

A COUPLE HOURS LATER, I'VE PARKED MY TRUCK ON THE street, eaten a surprisingly decent bowl of jambalaya, and suffered through some awkward-as-hell conversation.

"No drama in this household, babies. I know there's some tension here, but I don't want any theatrics unless they've been specifically orchestrated by yours truly." He looks over at me. "I heard about you and Abby Summers. I don't want that kind of crazy affecting my house or my business. She's the kinda lady who'd put a hole in your tire and whack off your member."

I grit my teeth and agree to keep his house drama-free.

Reese doesn't say anything.

In fact, she doesn't speak at all the entire time we eat.

After the terrible time that is dinner, I bring in some of my clothes and other necessities—things I'll need to keep inside—and try to avoid Reese.

A thump pulls me from my thoughts as she attempts to heft a box into the closet.

It's not a large box, but she struggles to lift it up above her head.

"Here." The word is clipped. I reach over her, shoving it onto the shelf. It's heavier than I thought. "What's in this thing?" I give it one last push and it slides into place.

"Books." Her voice is quiet.

"You can't keep those somewhere else? There's barely any room in here as it is."

Her back is to me, the line of her shoulders tense. I'm suddenly aware I'm blocking her in. I step back.

"Sorry," I mutter. I focus on putting clothes into the top drawer of the dresser but my eyes are drawn back over. She's hasn't moved. Still staring into the small closet like it has all the answers to our problems. Or maybe she's trying to determine if she can use it to flee into Narnia. I know the feeling.

Her hair is pulled from her face and for the first time I stop and look at her. Really look at her, in her cutoff shorts and plain red T-shirt, brown locks tied back into braids. Her features are small, dainty, delicate. Her jawline is fragile and yet somehow strong and determined even though her eyes are weary. And wary.

Said eyes lock with mine—a deep, dark blue that lures me in—and I yank my gaze away, heat creeping up my neck.

I clear my throat and fumble with getting the drawer shut. "Don't touch my stuff and I won't touch yours, got it?" Embarrassment makes my tone unnecessarily harsh. Again.

And now shame makes my stomach churn. The room constricts and the temperature in the cramped space increases ten degrees.

She's so weird. She hasn't spoken more than a few words since the whole agreement went down and she barely makes eye contact and something about her throws me off-balance, making everything I say sharp as a dagger.

She was witness to one of the worst moments of my life. It's like she can see every horrible thing about me and I can't do anything about it. Maybe I shouldn't take it out on her but it's like I can't control it.

She just turns away to reach into another box.

It irks, that she doesn't even respond to my harsh tone. Doesn't fight back. I could use a good row.

Abby would have my ass if I talked to her like that, and I would deserve it. Since we were kids, she's had no problem taking me to task, standing up for herself.

Reese is nothing like Abby.

Abby is brash, confident, tall, athletic. More likely to punch you in the face than hug you.

Reese is a little wisp of a thing, a mouse. More likely to run and hide than speak up.

Although . . . she didn't do so bad earlier. She didn't actually say much, but she's still here. She followed me despite my harsh words, she didn't leave when Jude issued his ridiculous terms, and she's still not cowed by me, even though I'm being a total dick. Momma would kill me if she could see me now.

"I'll . . . see you out there," I mumble, leaving the room and confusing thoughts about my new competitor behind.

Heading down the hall, I have to step out of the way

of some guys wheeling a couple of kegs in through the front door on a dolly.

The house is filling with random people.

“Jude won’t say what it is, man, just that it’s going to be a moneymaker,” a guy in a fraternity shirt says to someone on his cell as I pass by the living room.

Beast is at the counter in the kitchen, writing in his notebook. I stop next to him. “They don’t even know why they’re here?”

Beast stares at me but says nothing.

Does he ever speak? Or have a real name?

Voices and laughter and a strange humming filter in through the open window from the backyard.

I step out onto a recently stained wooden patio. The yard is larger than it looks like it would be from the front, stretching straight back for nearly an acre. Oak trees and giant bushes line the surrounding fence. There’s a pad of dirt in the way, way back and a swath of grass in the middle—covering almost the entire space.

On the patio directly in front of me sits an inflatable kiddie pool, about ten feet long and five feet wide, bright blue and covered in red cartoon dinosaurs.

The strange humming sound is whipped cream cans. People are lining up around the pool, filling it up. A pallet full of cans waits off to one side.

“No huffing the cans, babies!” Jude yells, overseeing the project.

I head in his direction. “What’s going on?”

“The first round of House Gladiators!” he proclaims, arms outstretched. Then he scratches his chin on a wince. “No, that’s not it. Room Tournament!” His arms lift again with the pronouncement.

I shake my head. “That’s terrible.”

“You’re right.” He sighs. “The Special Victors Squad!”

“Too much like special victims unit.” Although the most accurate of the choices so far.

He shrugs. “Probably.”

“Are you going to explain what’s up with the whipped cream?”

“You shall see, my friend.” He claps me on the back.

A throat clears.

Behind us, Reese stands silent and pale, her jaw firm. She does not look happy. She looks a little green, actually, if determined.

“I’m not getting naked.” Her voice wavers slightly.

“No worries, babies. This ain’t that kinda house. We are all about consent here. You keep your clothes on, put more on, take them all off, whatever you want. But you might want to put on something you don’t mind getting sticky. And you might consider having a beer. All drinks on the house for our . . . Roommate Death Battle Heroes of Doom!” The arms rise again.

Reese considers Jude with a frown. “You know, you don’t have to come up with something relating to a competition or event, necessarily. A name or title is effective enough if it describes the mood of what you’re attempting to produce. One good word can evoke the desired result.”

I blink at her. Is this the same person who followed

me here like an awkward puppy? I didn't know she could string so many words together.

Jude smiles at her, mustache twitching. "Oh yeah, smarty-pants? What would you suggest?"

"What about something like . . ." She thinks for a moment, her eyes narrowing in concentration. "Mischief, mayhem, chaos, pandemonium . . ." She murmurs a few more words, then stops, lifts her eyes. "Bedlam. Since we're fighting over an actual bed. And the term bedlam is derived from an actual historic asylum, Saint Mary Bethlehem in London."

"Huh." Jude tilts his head at her. "Not bad. Not bad at all."

She flushes and glances over at me, as if just realizing who she's talking to and what she's doing. "I have to go . . . clothes," she mumbles before disappearing inside.

I watch her leave. I can't figure her out. One minute as gawky as a newborn foal, the next spouting SAT words like a walking thesaurus.

"Drink?" Jude asks, pulling my focus away from the open sliding door where Reese disappeared.

"No. Gotta stay focused for," I glance down at the cream-filled kiddie pool, "whatever this is."

"Good call." Jude nods at me, then jogs over to the keg.

My eyes track him and stop on a familiar blonde head that matches my own.

"Annabel?" What the hell is my sister doing here?

We lock eyes and then move toward each other, weaving through the crowd.

"What are you doing here?" she asks.

"I was about to ask you the same thing. I'm here because I have nowhere to live and now I've gotten sucked into some kind of competition for housing."

She clucks in sympathy. "How are you feeling?"

"I'm okay, just tired and of course I'm still upset about . . . Wait a minute. Don't try and change the subject. What are you doing here? You graduated, remember? And college parties have never exactly been in your wheelhouse."

She glances around and then takes my arm, pulling me over to the side of the yard, away from where most of the people are congregating. "I'm here for a story."

"A story about what?"

"Not at liberty to say at the moment."

I roll my eyes. "You're a reporter for the *Daily Blue*, not the *New York Times*."

"So? I have some integrity, you know. Why don't you tell me what's going on here tonight?"

"I don't know much. Just that I've got to compete with someone for a room here." I nod toward the house.

"How much do you know about the owner of the house?"

"Jude?"

She nods.

I search the yard and find him over by the keg, cat robe swaying while he gesticulates wildly to a few people. Beast looms behind him, setting up some kind of stage-lighting tower. "I never met him until today. Why? What do you know about him?"

"Nothing. That's why I'm asking you, you dolt. Who are you competing against?"

"Some other college student." Should I mention she's also Abby's former roommate? Maybe not. I don't want to hear Annabel rant and rave about Abby again.

Instead, I glance around to see if Reese has come back yet. I finally spot her in the opposite corner of the yard, watching people mill about. She's still wearing her cutoff shorts but she's changed into a large yellow T-shirt. She glances around and then takes a big step back, disappearing into some hedges. Literally, she's hiding in the bushes.

So weird.

"There," I nod in her direction. "Two o'clock."

Annabel searches the yard, then lifts her brows at me. "The one in the bushes?" She laughs. "All I can see is hair."

"Yep."

"Huh. This will be very interesting. You'll have to introduce me."

Before I can give her an emphatic *hell to the no*, Jude jumps on the deck with a megaphone in one hand.

"Thank you everyone for being here." His voice booms out over the assembled crowd. People inside file out into the backyard. "The books are about to open and you will have fifteen minutes to finalize your bets. I know you are all aquiver in antici . . . pation."

He grins as the crowd groans.

"So, let me give you a little taste of what we're cooking here tonight. We have one room available at

Casa de Jude and two people vying for a chance to be my roommate. Can you blame them? I mean, look at me." He poses suggestively, opening one side of his cat-covered robe to reveal a surprisingly ripped chest.

Jeering laughter fills the yard and a masculine voice yells, "I'd do you!"

"I know, babies, I know. Calm yourselves. What we have planned here is a series of events spanning over the next two weeks, starting tonight. It will be Jude Parker's *Bedlam*!"

There are some whistles and half-hearted applause.

"We have two competitors who will be engaging in a battle of will, brains, strength, and cunning to see who will qualify to live at this humble abode." He gestures to the house behind him.

"You, my lovely babies, will be given the opportunity to choose who you think will emerge victorious right before each game begins. I will not be disclosing the details of each challenge until the betting books have filled so choose wisely. I'm glad you all showed up tonight because there will be only one chance, tonight, after our first match, to bet on who will be our ultimate champion at the end of all seven games. The winner will be determined here, in this exact spot, in exactly two weeks."

He's got the crowd interested now, everyone focused and alert.

"Without further ado, let me present our challengers. Front and center, we have our first competitor." He points at me, and a blinding spotlight flicks on, pointed straight at my face. I cover my eyes but it's too late. I sense more than see the eyes of the crowd swing in my direction since I'm still blinking away the brightness. Jude keeps speaking into the megaphone, like he's suddenly turned into the "let's get ready to rumble" announcer. "Standing at six foot two, 170 pounds of lean muscle, this fighter is a beast on the track and not too shabby in the classroom. Known for his perseverance and determination even in the face of unbeatable odds and questionable ex-girlfriends, I give you Mr. Fitz Moreland!"

There are some cheers and catcalls and once the sound peters out, Jude keeps going.

"In the north corner, standing in a bush over there, may I present the competition." The light leaves my face and heads over to the hedges. She startles at the bright beam of attention and her face immediately flushes pink, but she stands straighter and crosses her arms over her chest. "Don't let that meek demeanor fool you, babies. This tiny lady has a mind like a steel trap and a hidden, but emerging sense of self-preservation that may be the cinch in this race. May I present to you Ms. Reese Jackson, daughter of the famed Jackson artists!" Scattered applause and murmurs meet his announcement.

Reese's parents are *the* Jacksons? They don't show their faces very often, but everyone knows who they are.

How did Jude know? I doubt Reese offered up the information.

"The bets start now, so give your money to Beast." Jude bows with a flourish and exits the patio.

"I'll see you after," Annabel tells me before disappearing into the crowd, where people are forming a haphazard line.

I find my eyes drawn once again to Reese. Over by the bushes. Alone.

Once again, a flicker of shame and guilt wiggles through me.

I've been rude to her since last night. My momma would skin my hide if she knew how I was behaving toward a lady. Or toward anyone.

And with that thought, my feet carry me to the corner of the yard, where she's watching the revelry with a blank face.

The moment she sees me coming, her whole body goes rigid and she looks down at the ground, like she can will herself invisible if she only concentrates hard enough.

"Hey." I stop next to her.

She doesn't respond and we stand in silence while uneasy tension builds a stony wall between us.

I clear my throat. "What do you think we're gonna have to do?" I ask, for lack of anything else to say.

"If I knew, I wouldn't tell you." The words are rude, but her tone is just matter-of-fact.

"Fair enough."

I should walk away. We barely know each other and what we do know we don't apparently like, but maybe I should try to get to know something about her. Maybe that will help me defeat her. Find her weak spots. Or something.

The thoughts make me frown. I've never been good at scheming.

I watch the crowd with her, wanting to speak but also not wanting to be the first to break the silence.

The yard is full of people milling around the keg, laughing, flirting. The line for the betting dwindles until there are only a couple left.

"Hey!" One of the last people in line, a brunette in a sorority shirt, jumps and pushes at the guy behind her. "Keep your hands to yourself, asshole!"

"I'm just messing around," the guy says, loud enough to get the attention of half the people in the yard.

Beast reaches out, picks up the guy by the collar of his polo shirt with one meaty paw, and dangles him in the air. "Put me down!" the guy yells, legs kicking. "I didn't do nothing!"

Jude's voice booms out over his megaphone, echoing over the crowd. "Now listen here, sir. We live by a code of gentlemanly behavior around these parts. There will be no getting handsy unless it's agreed upon with enthusiastic, affirmative consent."

He gives a short nod to Beast, who's still holding the guy by the scruff. He turns and walks around the corner of the house. The handsy guy keeps yelling even after they disappear, but it's mostly drowned out by the rest of the crowd's clapping.

I huff a surprised laugh. I don't think I've ever been to a party quite like this. Reese is pressing her lips together, holding back a smile.

Our eyes meet and a small crack forms in the wall of tension between us.

Beast returns—alone—and finishes getting the final bets in. Then Jude gets the crowd's attention once again with his megaphone.

"It's time to reveal the details of tonight's shenanigans. As you can see, we have here a pool full of whipped cream. Hiding somewhere inside are two pieces of bubble gum. The challenge for our competitors will be to locate the gum in the pool. The first person to find a piece and blow a bubble will be our day-one winner. The catch . . ." His eyes find ours. "You cannot use your hands."

Reese's lips are pressed into a white line, her face even paler than before.

I put a hand on her arm. "It will be okay," I murmur.

She looks at my hand and then pulls away, not meeting my eyes. "It would be better if we weren't friends."

Maybe Jude's right. Not as weak as she seems.

"Fine." I stalk toward the pool, ignoring the brush of disappointment at her words. She's right. We are in a competition.

Jude stages us on either side of the pool, then hands us each a set of goggles. I pull mine on and watch through the wavy lenses as Reese struggles to yank hers over her braids.

"Are we *ready*?" he yells into the megaphone, riling up the crowd.

Cheers and whoops and hollers fill the air.

"It begins with one blow." He holds up the whistle.

"Title of your sex tape!" someone in the crowd calls out, instigating a chorus of groans and laughter.

"All right, all right, you animals." Jude waves a hand to shush them. He turns and meets my eyes, then his gaze switches to Reese. "Ready?" he asks in a low volume.

We nod.

"Set," he says louder.

I keep my gaze on Jude as he lifts the metal whistle to his mouth.

The shrill sound pierces the air.

Reese shocks me by flinging herself full force into the pool, sending foam flying, faster than a bee-stung stallion.

The surprise puts me at a disadvantage and I dive in a split second after her.

Just before white fluff covers my goggles, I get a flash of her determined face, eyes closed, mouth chomping, body twisting like a champ.

I was not expecting her to be so aggressive. I want to laugh but if I don't focus, I'm gonna end up on the couch tonight.

I can't see anything. The goggles might be protecting my irises from sugar overload but the plastic is quickly coated in goop. I know I can't use my hands, but he said nothing about feet. I feel around, wiggling the rest of my body into the pool, concentrating on the sensations and attempting to locate the piece of gum.

The space is small—no more than five or six feet

across. My long limbs are already squished and I get the occasional jab from Reese. Mostly unintentional . . . I think. Except for one hard, purposeful knee to the ribs.

It doesn't hurt, it makes me smile.

I didn't think she had it in her.

And then it's there, a small rock-like object near my knee. I twist in the pool to bring my face toward it.

There. Near Reese's waist.

My head hits her ribs but I can't help it. I latch on to the gum, getting a knee in the head for my efforts.

I sit up out of the pool with the prize in my mouth, chewing fast.

It's hard as granite. What the hell?

My goggles are nearly impossible to see through, but I can make out the dark outline of Reese as she sits up too, chomping on her own tough piece of gum like it's her last meal and she's half starved.

But she's too late.

I blow and a small bubble emerges.

Jude immediately lifts one of my arms into the air, like we're in a boxing ring instead of a kiddie pool covered in cartoon dinosaurs.

"And the winner by a bubble yummy is Fitz Moreland!" he yells into the megaphone.

The crowd is cheering and I still can't see anything. I use my free hand to wipe my face and yank off the goggles.

Jude hands me the key to the room, a small piece of metal hanging from a thick gold chain.

I pull it over my head and glance down at Reese,

who's still sitting in the pool, covered in sticky white cream, looking like ten miles of a bad road.

"Hey."

She looks up at me, a drowned kitten.

She's kinda cute, actually, even with her hair sticking up in a crazy mess of dark ripples and spikes.

"Fitz, introduce me to your competition." Then Annabel is there, standing on the other side of the pool and smiling at Reese like she's her new best friend.

I sigh. "Reese, this is my sister. I apologize in advance for anything she says or does or doesn't do. Or anything at all, really."

"Shut it, pool boy. Here, I brought you a towel."

Of course, it's not for me. She hands it to Reese, who accepts the gesture gratefully and steps out of the kiddie pool, wrapping the towel around her narrow shoulders.

Before I can make any comments, Annabel drags Reese off toward the house, talking a mile a minute.

What is she up to?

5

ou'll never do a whole lot unless you're brave enough to try.

—Dolly Parton

Reese

Annabel isn't like anyone I've ever met. For one, she's helpful. She clears a direct path through the line to the bathroom, allowing me to get rinsed off without having to wait around in sticky misery.

And then when I get out, wrapped only in a robe, she's waiting with the room key in hand so I can get in and change into clean clothes.

It's a relief when I'm safely ensconced in the small space. Alone. I've had more than I can take of socializing for one day.

I can't even believe what just happened. I jumped into a pool full of whipped cream in front of a crowd of people. With Fitz Moreland.

And that's not all. I lost.

Lost.

And I was so close.

I should have tried harder. I can beat any task with a little effort and perseverance, even something as asinine as searching for gum in a tub full of whipped cream.

I pull one of my old shirts from the bag Granny made me take, a bright red T-shirt with a crow on the front, the word *nevermore* sketched above it.

I wore it my first day at Blue Falls High and then never again.

There's a knock at the door. "Reese? Are you dressed?"

Annabel is out there. And she still has the key. She could come in if she wanted.

"Uh . . . almost." With no time to search for something else, I tug the shirt over my head and then grab a clean pair of pants from the dresser, throwing them on with haste.

I unlock the door and open it.

Annabel smiles and steps into the room, closing the door and dampening the noise from the rest of the house.

"So, this is it, huh?" She glances around. "All this work for a space smaller than a cell block."

"It's better than the street."

"True."

The resemblance between Fitz and Annabel is strong. They both have oval-shaped faces, gold-tinted hair, and chocolate-brown eyes. Annabel isn't as wiry as Fitz though. Fitz is all lean muscle and rugged masculinity.

Annabel is . . . something else. Voluptuous. Wide, smiling mouth, red lipstick. She's one of those girls who can pull off wearing wrap dresses, like she is tonight. A simple black dress with ballet flats. I'd look like a beanpole in curtains.

"I love your shirt."

I glance down in surprise. "You do?"

"I love Poe. Did you know he wrote more comedy than horror?"

"Yes. Only fifteen out of about seventy stories were of the darker variety." And before I can stop it, my mouth runs away with me. "Poe is largely remembered because a nemesis spread false accounts of him after his death, painting Poe as someone with a dark and hedonistic history. He wasn't, and it backfired and made Poe even more of a legend."

My favorite factoid. I stop and brace myself for an odd glance and a quick departure.

But Annabel surprises me. "Ah, yes. Rufus Wilmot Griswold."

I blink. "Yes."

She didn't look at me funny and run away; she actually knows about Poe too and doesn't think it's odd to spout random facts during a conversation.

She sits on the edge of the bed. "I was named after one of his poems, Annabel Lee."

My mouth pops open in surprise. "That's so cool."

"You think so?" Her nose wrinkles.

"I would love to be named after a literary figure," I say with feeling, sitting next to her on the bed. "I was named after my mother's favorite candy."

She laughs. "So, tell me about yourself. You from Blue Falls?" Her eyes are curious, not spiteful or mean, and her tone is interested and friendly, like she actually wants to talk to me. I'm still wary. But there's no passive-aggressive politeness to her words, unlike everyone else I've met, including her brother, who seems to hate every second in my company. Except for earlier when he was trying to be nice. Probably so he could suss out my weak spots for eventual attack and pillage.

"Yes. I was born here."

Her head tilts. "Huh. I've never seen you around."

"That's intentional."

She grins. "Were you homeschooled or what?"

"For a time. I started at Blue Falls High sophomore year."

She watches me, lips pursed. "I really hope you win this whole competition thing."

My brows lift to my hairline. "But Fitz is your brother."

She shrugs. "Little brother. By three years."

"He's still family," I point out.

"He's a pain in the ass. Besides, this whole situation is good for him."

"Why do you say that?"

"Because his heretofore blissful existence has basically been shattered. I mean, come on, Reese. If you're from here and you went to Blue Falls High, you know how Fitz and Abby are. Or were, I guess. He thought she was the most important thing in his life, and now he's seeing her for what she truly is. Now maybe he can move on and be happy. I don't think he even realizes how unhappy he's been."

I'm not sure how to respond. She's talking so openly and I'm not used to having candid conversations like this with someone I barely know.

"Maybe I can help you, even. If the opportunity arises."

"You want to help me beat him?"

"Yes."

"You want him to lose."

"Sometimes losing is better than winning. You can't grow without a little pain."

A faint glimmer of guilt moves through me. Conspiring with Fitz's sister to make him lose? I would feel terrible if Scarlett pitted herself against me. On the other hand, it's not my fault Annabel is offering her assistance, just like it's not my fault Fitz is having a hard go of it.

I'm a victim of circumstance. As a matter of fact, he triggered all of this to begin with.

I firm my resolve with a nod. "Right. How, exactly, are you going to help me?"

She shrugs. "I haven't quite figured that part out yet.

But it won't hurt to have someone in your corner, don't you think?"

THE SLAM OF A DOOR YANKS ME FROM THE ONLY HOUR OF sleep I've gotten all night.

The couch is worse than *not good.*

Not good is an understatement of gigantic proportions.

Scientific notation would be necessary to quantify how awful it is.

The noise-canceling headphones don't help when people don't see you and accidently sit on your face. Which has happened more than once. And I don't think always accidently.

I rub my gritty eyes and reach for my cell phone to check the time. Did I set the alarm?

It's 7:36. "Holy scatterplot."

I have exactly twenty-four minutes to make it to class.

Leaping from the couch, I race to the bathroom, nearly tripping on Mr. Bojangles asleep and splayed out in the middle of the hallway, belly exposed, perfectly content and unconcerned with my struggles.

I only take the time to pee and splash my face with cold water. I left my book bag in the room and I don't even attempt silence, throwing the door open and then rummaging through the closet for the stuff I stashed there last night.

It doesn't matter. The door is unlocked, which means

Fitz is gone. The bed is neatly made. He probably slept like a baby and flitted out the door to the sound of songbirds while forest creatures helped him dress.

All the more reason to hate him.

I throw on an old tie-dyed T-shirt and jeans.

I've nearly made it to the front door when a looming presence appears in the kitchen doorway and I gasp before I realize who it is.

Beast.

For someone so large, he moves like a ninja. Or an ambush predator.

His giant hands hold out coffee in a disposable cup and a small brown paper sack. I take the items and peek inside the bag. There's a neatly wrapped sandwich next to an apple.

I meet his eyes with a surprised blink. "Thank you."

A slow nod is my only response.

Then I'm out the door, blowing down the sidewalk along with the dead leaves from the trees finally catching up with the change in seasons, even though it's already over seventy degrees.

I didn't have a chance to grab a hair tie, and the wind whips my hair all over the place.

The house isn't far from campus, but I'm never late and I already missed a full day.

"Hi," a voice calls in passing, but I don't look over.

I've made the mistake of waving or returning salutations, only to discover they were inevitably attempting to communicate with someone else nearby.

"Hey." Now from someone coming in the other direction. This time, I glance around. No one else in the immediate vicinity. Must have been some kind of mistake.

It's not until I've reached the building where my calculus class is held that I have a minute to catch my breath.

The auditorium-style classroom is nearly full, but I make it through the door with only a minute to spare and take my normal spot in the very back.

I toss my bag at my feet and bend over to pull out my materials while trying to get my breathing under control.

While I'm still in a supine position, I catch someone sitting next to me out of the corner of my eye.

Unusual in and of itself, but even odder is the fact that when I sit up and meet his eyes, he's smiling.

At me.

"Hi." Dark hair, scruffy jaw, flannel shirt. Vaguely familiar.

And he's talking. To me. There can be no mistake this time, his eyes are fixed on mine and there's no one on my other side. I look twice to make sure.

But people don't do this. People don't notice me. Ever.

What is happening?

"Hi," I reply. My face is already heating. I'm so unused to talking to fellow students, it's actually making me blush. I take a slow breath. I can do this. I can talk to people I don't know.

I can be normal.

Maybe.

"You did a great job last night," he says.

"Oh. Thank you?" The heat in my face increases. He was there?

"I'm betting on you next time, so don't let me down." He lifts his fist.

I stare at it. I've seen people fist bump before, but I've never actually done it.

Before I can think about it too much, I tap my clenched fist against his. The gesture is unpracticed and graceless, but my classmate doesn't seem to care too much.

His response is a slow grin, exposing a dimple on one cheek. "I'm Duke."

I nod. "Reese."

"I know," he says.

Class starts.

I turn my attention to the front and try to ignore the presence of Duke while I take notes and listen to the lecture.

I guess I'm not so invisible anymore.

But I am exhausted from the lack of sleep. So much so, I nearly doze off, jerking awake when Duke stands up next to me.

"See ya, sleepy." He laughs and takes off.

I blink. Everyone is moving. Class is over. Still a little fuzzy, I gather all my items and head down the steps to the front of the auditorium.

~

Relief soars through me when I get back to Jude's after my last class and no one else is home.

Without another thought, I immediately collapse on the bed in the little room in utter exhaustion.

I don't care if Fitz won the game last night. It's daytime and he's not using the bed now, so it's mine.

Between the lack of sleep over the last couple of days and all the socialization, I'm drained. I conk out so hard I don't emerge from my sleep cocoon until darkness is falling.

I'm not sure what brings me out of my slumber, whether it's the dull sound of voices outside the door or the sensation that I'm not alone.

Either way, I blink my eyes open to find a figure standing in the middle of the darkening room.

Gasping, I jolt upright, heart pounding, brain still foggy from sleep.

"What?" I ask to the room in general.

"Sorry." It's Fitz. He clicks on the light and the Christmas bulbs fill the space with subtle illumination. "I didn't know you were in here."

"How long have you been standing there?"

Was he watching me sleep?

Should I be flattered or offended? I reach a hand up to correct my mangled ponytail and wipe away any drool.

Offended. Definitely offended.

"I just got home. I had track practice so I need to change."

I focus on him. He's wearing a Blue Falls athletic tank top and running shorts. "Right. Sorry."

Wait, why am I apologizing? I hate him. Also, he didn't really answer my question.

I hop off the bed, suddenly embarrassed to be lying in a bed with a guy looming over me. I fidget with my rumpled clothes and chaotic hair and we stand in strained silence until we both move at once, me in the direction of the door and him toward the dresser, the small space making it impossible to avoid brushing against each other.

His skin is still hot from the sun. He smells like masculine deodorant and fresh air.

"Sorry," he mutters.

He's apologized twice—and me once—during this conversation, which makes me feel somewhat better about myself, in a petty and vindictive way.

Once I'm in the hall, he shuts the door with a thud and I stand there for a second, not quite ready to leave the quiet emptiness of the hallway, still trying to wake up and gather my thoughts.

He shuffles around inside the room. The dresser opens and shuts. Is he getting undressed?

I blink away thoughts of what he might look like under the tank top. All lean torso and corded muscles.

If I were a renaissance man like da Vinci, I would sculpt him.

Stop, Reese. He's lower than a snake fart.

But my wayward thoughts don't have a chance of being squashed, because the door opens and Fitz steps out and now it's gotten so much worse because he's not wearing any shirt at all and my imaginings are nothing compared to the sight of Fitz Moreland bare chested and only in running shorts.

Broad shoulders—broader than I realized, or maybe it just looks that way since he's so close I could lean forward and taste him—taper down to a trim waist. It's not quite a six-pack, but near enough that I can't stop staring and—

"What are you doing?"

"Um. Nothing." Mortification floods through me like a tsunami.

I turn on a sharp heel and walk down the hall.

Awkwardland. It's where I live. And I'm the president, mayor, and sole citizen.

I shake off the embarrassment. Nothing is wrong with me. I'm simply having a normal, human reaction to an attractive potential mate. Just like in the animal kingdom. And I've never felt more animalistic than I do at the current moment, but it's nothing I can't control, it's biology.

He's the enemy, and I'd do best to remember it.

6

Real courage . . . is when you know you're licked before you begin, but you begin anyway and you see it through no matter what.

—Harper Lee

Fitz

There's no challenge tonight, but a group of people are gathered somewhere in the house. Occasional laughter, clapping, and shouting can be heard even with the door shut.

At least it's not as crowded as it was last night, which is a blessing. I have homework to do. Jude clearly doesn't need to worry about school, but Beast has class. I've seen him around campus. He's hard to miss.

After I shower off the sweat from practice, I try to get

some work done in the room, but I'm starving and the bed isn't very comfortable for sitting and working on my computer. After hunching over for almost an hour, I give up and head out to the kitchen.

Making my way through the living area, I get a look at Jude's guests. They aren't college students. They're all over sixty, at least.

Jude is right in the thick of it too, laughing and passing around trays of appetizers while Mr. Bojangles sits in his lap, regarding the goings-on like a king lording over his subjects.

As soon as I step into the kitchen, Beast hands me a steaming bowl of food along with a fork and napkin.

"Thanks." I take the bowl. Smells good. Some kind of meat, vegetable, rice concoction.

How did he know I was coming?

Beast covers the casserole dish, puts it in the fridge, then walks silently out the doorway into the living room, where I can still hear voices and laughter.

Does he ever speak, even to Jude? I haven't heard him utter more than a grunt since moving in.

I turn toward the dining table and that's when I spot her.

Reese. Alone, laptop open in front of her, typing away at warp speed.

It's going to be an uncomfortable couple of weeks if we can't be civil to each other in close proximity. Especially after the odd moments both inside and outside the room before I went to shower.

I didn't mean to creep on her sleeping, and she woke

up right as I was about to announce my presence anyway.

Then outside the door, I could swear she was checking me out before she ran away.

It was . . . really flattering, actually.

So flattering it led to a very pleasurable shower.

Maybe this means we can be friends, at least? Attraction leads to . . . peace treaty? Maybe it's a stretch, but there's only one way to find out. I make my way to the table and pull out a chair.

I'll probably get the freeze-out. Again. But no one will be able to say I didn't give it my best shot.

"Hey."

Reese isn't watching me, her eyes resolutely on her computer screen. There's a textbook next to her and a dirty dish set to the side, forgotten.

I glance at the cover of her textbook. "Quantum physics?"

She nods.

Well, at least that's some kind of acknowledgement. "Isn't that a third-year class?"

She shrugs.

It's not actual verbal conversation, but I suppose it's an improvement over a complete snub.

I sit across from her and take a few bites of food while I decide how to approach this.

"Listen, Reese," I wipe my mouth with the napkin, "I'm really sorry about how things started out with us and everything. I said a lot of things that were hurtful. I shouldn't have placed the blame on you for this . . . situation."

She blinks at me, her eyes wide and hyperfocused on me like she can read my actual thoughts.

Don't think about sex.

Heat creeps up my neck.

Her stare *is* sort of erotic, in an intense-pixie kind of way. And she's wearing a thin white T-shirt that reveals the outline of her bra underneath and I have to force my eyes to remain fixed on hers.

"You're right," she says finally.

What were we talking about?

I wait for her to say more, maybe apologize for her own rude behavior, or maybe scold me for inappropriate thoughts, but she turns back to her work.

I stay at the table, eating my food in silence, which actually isn't as tense as I thought it would be.

Shouts and laughter and clapping echo from the living room.

"What are they doing in there?" I ask.

She doesn't answer for so long I think I'm being shunned again, but then finally, "They're watching *Antiques Roadshow*."

"Uh, you mean that program on PBS where people have their old junk valued?"

"Yep. Jude has them make their bets when each item is first presented. They have to guess how much it's worth, and whoever gets closest to the actual value wins the pot."

"Huh."

I keep eating as she keeps typing, and I relax into the silence. It's better than I thought it would be. The sounds of conversation continue to trickle in from the living room and Reese's gentle tapping on her computer is actually kind of soothing and the food is pretty damn delicious.

And then my phone rings and it's my mother.

I've been dreading her call. I don't want to lie, even by omission, but I can't ignore her either.

"Hey, Momma." I stand up from the table and take my bowl to the sink.

"Hey, baby boy. How is school?"

"It's great." The words are like dust in my mouth. I grab a glass from the cupboard and fill it.

"How's Abby doing? I was talking to Martha earlier and she wanted me to tell you to have Abby call her. Would you let her know? I know you kids are real busy, but she's starting to worry. And you know how Abby gets. If things aren't right in front of her she forgets they exist."

My stomach churns, the food suddenly a lump of lead in my belly. I take a long drink of water before I respond. "She's fine. I'll tell her to call." *Or not.*

Maybe I can text Abby or have someone from the team pass along the message for me. Not necessarily a lie.

She keeps up a steady stream of conversation while I wash my dish, asking about my grades and track and if I'm getting enough sleep and brushing my teeth. Typical mom stuff.

Then after a small silence, when I think we might be done, she drops the bomb. "I wanted to let you know we're selling the house."

"What? Why?"

I grew up in that house. Granted, it's not any kind of mansion, just a modest one story out on the south side of town. Not quite middle class, not quite the worst neighborhood in town. But I can't believe they would sell their home of over twenty years.

"Well, your grandma is getting a lot older now and since she's living alone down there in Florida, it's about time your father and I went to stay with her."

"Is everything okay?"

"Everything's fine, baby. It's just her hip is bad, you know. Now that you kids are out of the house, there's nothing to really keep us here. We're gonna get more than three times what we paid for this place. And with your father being off work now a few months, it's not looking like he's going to be able to go back." The last sentence streams by, like getting it out fast will make it hurt any less.

"But he's going to be okay, right?" A get a flash in my head, a memory of when I was young and he used to lift me up and fly me around like Superman. He was so strong, I thought he could never be anything else.

"He'll be all right. Now don't be worrying about us. We'll be okay. He's gonna have to take early retirement, but that means we've got to cut back. I already called Annabel and let her know. I need you kids to come by soon and get some of your stuff. Scott will let you store a few boxes at his place, right?"

"Uh." Shit. More lies. But she's stressed enough, I can't go making it worse. "Yeah, I'm sure it's no problem." Jude has a garage. There's got to be somewhere for me to keep a few boxes. If not . . . well, I'll figure something out.

A few minutes later, we hang up and I turn away from the sink to find Reese still sitting at the table, watching me.

I had forgotten she was there.

"Is everything okay? With your dad?"

She heard my whole conversation. And I'm a little annoyed she's asking. *Now* she wants to be cordial?

I swallow back the harsh retort that wants to escape.

"He's fine," I say instead, and then I leave her to her studies.

TWENTY-FOUR HOURS LATER, THE CROWD AT JUDE'S IS ONCE again near capacity. It was Reese's turn to make dinner: macaroni and cheese with cut-up hot dogs. Not exactly a gourmet meal from the person who tried to use the fact she could cook as a bargaining chip, but the food is filling enough. We haven't talked since the night before, since our days are full of classes and schoolwork, and I spent what was left of my afternoon pounding out my frustrations on the all-weather track next to the football stadium.

Track has never been something I've loved, but I'm

good at it. All you need is heart. Determination. Nothing else really matters. It was my ticket to getting an education and helping my parents.

But now they're moving anyway.

After I eat and shower, I head out to the backyard. On my way, I pass Beast in the living room, notebook in his hand, silent amongst a crowd of arguing frat-boy types while they place their bets.

No kiddie pool this time, thankfully. This time a significant portion of the grass is covered by a large, dark tarp. I circle around a group of people gathered on the patio, trying to get an idea of what Jude has set up this time.

Once I get closer, it becomes apparent that a game board has been painted onto the tarp. The tarp is littered with toddler-size plastic ladders and slides. It's a life-size Chutes and Ladders game. At the end, a giant macramé key tilts onto one side. At the top of the game board, someone has painted *Bedlam* in a giant, red curlicue script.

What the heck are we gonna do with this?

"You got the key?" Jude materializes next to me. He's wearing another Jude-style dark velvet robe. But instead of cats, there are goats. Miniature goats frolicking around.

"Yeah." I pull it from around my neck and hand it to him.

"You 'bout ready?"

"As ready as I'll ever be. Reese here yet?"

He shrugs, nonchalant as ever. "She's hiding somewhere."

I smile, but there's no opportunity to comment on Reese's ninja-like disappearing ability.

Jude turns to face the crowd, lifting his megaphone to his face. "All right, babies, listen up!" He waits for the chatter to settle down before continuing. "Tonight's challenge is a board game we all know and love—with a twist. Tonight, it will be all about the brains."

Someone in the crowd yells, "*Braaaaains*!"

"No, it's not a zombie hunt, although that would be a mighty fine idea. I'm talking about a trivia challenge, Bedlam style! Our players will begin at the start square." Using a small stack of notecards in his hand, he points to the starting square. "The goal is to make it to the key at the end. I will be asking each player trivia questions, and if they answer correctly, they move forward a spot. If they answer wrong, their opponent will have the opportunity to answer. If the opposing player answers correctly, they will move forward *two* spaces."

Reese shows up then, stopping next to me. I offer her a smile, but she gives me the dead eye and turns her focus to Jude.

"Our chutes and ladders," he points them out, "are just like the board game. You reach a square with a ladder, you follow it up. You reach a square with a slide, follow it down and backward in the game. Any questions?"

"What's Beast's real name?" someone yells.

"I don't know, why don't you ask him?" Jude drawls,

eliciting scattered laughter. He smiles indulgently at the crowd, then turns to us. "Fitz, since you are the reigning champ, you're up first. Are we all ready?"

The crowd yells.

Reese and I nod.

"Fitz. What color are aircraft black boxes?"

Is this a trick question? I have no idea. "Black?"

"Wrong." A harsh buzzer fills the air. "Reese?" Jude nods at her.

"Orange," she answers, her eyes sliding to mine.

A loud *ding ding ding* sounds.

"Correct. You get to move forward two spaces."

She takes two steps forward onto the game board amidst some scattered applause and whoops.

"Alrighty then, Reese. This next question is for you. In 1960, which country became the first in the world to have a female prime minister?"

"Sri Lanka." She answers with zero hesitation.

I can't help but stare at her in surprise. How does she know these things?

"Correct. You get to move forward one, and oh, look at that you get to take the ladder up as well."

There are some groans and a mixture of claps from the crowd.

"Fitz." Jude turns back to me. "What is the collective name for a group of crows?"

Finally. Something I know. "A murder."

Scattered applause. I move forward one.

The game goes on like this. I get a few correct but miss most of them. Reese misses nothing.

Ever.

I almost think I have a chance when she has to take a slide back to the prior row of spaces, but then I get hammered in a series of questions about which I know nothing and Reese, of course, knows every single one.

In which country was the Caesar salad invented? Mexico.

What is the tiny plastic tip covering the end of a shoelace called? An aglet.

What is the dot over a lowercase *i* and *j* called? A tittle.

A tittle?

"I just wanted to hear our innocent little Reese here say tit," Jude admits.

She handily makes it to the end, where the giant key awaits.

Jude lifts her arm, announces her the Bedlam winner of the second challenge, and hands her the key.

A tall guy on the sideline approaches Reese, smiling and excited.

They bump fists and she says something I can't make out over all the chatter. They laugh together.

He's eyeballing her like he's one of the Bumpuses' dogs and she's a ripe turkey on Christmas morning. She's flushed and smiling and I've never seen her look happy. Her eyes are bright, her face glowing, and she's . . . pretty. Like *really* pretty.

Tall guy is still talking to her, focused and leaning into her space. He's got one of those butt chins.

I hate guys with butt chins.

"Stop frowning." Jude stops beside me.

"I'm not frowning."

"Yes, you are. Don't frown. You get another shot at the key in a couple days. On Begonia Day!" He laughs and claps me on the back before turning his attention to the crowd. "Babies, listen up! As you all know, Saturday is my favorite day of the year: Begonia Day."

There are scattered claps and catcalls.

Blue Falls has to be the only university that celebrates their mascot's birthday each year with a giant party. There are carnival food and games and giant inflatable obstacle courses. All proceeds go to various charities, and there are booths and such set up on the quad next to the festivities. Begonia is our mascot, the fighting boar, although she's not actually a boar. Just a regular pig. They keep her in a large pen and barn on campus, probably the most spoiled pig in the whole country.

Jude continues, "We'll meet on the steps of the library at ten a.m. sharp to issue the next challenge. Our score is now one to one!" He rubs his mustache. "Anticipate more tomfoolery and a lot more ballyhoo."

His speech over, the crowd slowly disperses, people heading inside or over to where the keg is set up. Some leave around the side of the house. Music kicks on and the party swings into gear.

I decide to check out my sofa slash bed for the night and get some stuff out of the room before Reese locks herself in there. I make it to the door right as she's using the key to unlock it.

"I need to grab a couple things."

She hesitates but then nods before opening the door and letting me enter first.

"Thanks." I grab my clothes and backpack along with my track clothes and shoes.

She's standing next to the door, arms crossed over her chest, looking everywhere but at me.

I clear my throat and she finally meets my eyes. "Nice work out there."

She hesitates, as if waiting for me to say more, then mutters, "Thanks."

I shift my shoes and clothes to my left hand and stick out my right in her direction, knowing I'll probably be rebuffed but going for it anyway. "You're a worthy opponent. I know we're competing, but I still want you to know I admire your intelligence. How did you know all of those things?"

"I read a lot." I don't think she's going to take my olive branch, but finally, she slips her hand in mine, small and soft, though her shake is firm. "I haven't decided if you're worthy yet or not."

I chuckle. "Probably not."

Her head cocks. "I'll try to reserve any harsh judgment until it's been warranted from this point out, if you'll do the same."

For some reason, her begrudging cease-fire feels like a win, even though I lost. I can't stop the grin spreading across my face. "You're on."

7

There is no shortcut in life. You have to take it one step at a time and work hard. And you have to give back.

—Hank Aaron

Fitz

"You ready for Begonia Day?" Jude nudges me in the shoulder.

I grunt and shovel a spoon of Cap'n Crunch in my mouth.

I'm too tired to give full word responses.

Jude, however, is bouncing around next to me on the couch like a tween who's won Fortnite.

He's been like this for an hour. The man is a

machine. He never seems to sleep and yet has endless energy.

I need to focus. I have to win the competition today. I have a major track meet tomorrow—and I'm dreading it. Not only will I probably run into Abby, my teammates are going to kill me if I slack during the relay. Not to mention, if I don't place at least in the top three consistently, they probably won't renew my scholarship.

"You're way cranky pants," Jude says, his tone amiable.

I grunt again.

"Oh no, my friend, we mustn't dwell," Jude recites dramatically. "No, not today. We can't." His hand splays on his chest. "Not on Begonia Day!" He bounces on the cushion again, making the milk slosh in my bowl. I give him the evil eye.

"Oh, this is the best part." He smacks me on the shoulder, making my spoon jump and cereal fall in my lap. "Matthew McConaughey is the man."

On the screen, the actor is navigating a sailboat on the open water and flirting with a blonde. "If you say so."

"I do say so. Any man who plays the bongos naked is someone I can relate to."

I finish my breakfast and we keep watching while Matt goes rock climbing with his buddies and inevitably talks about his love interest.

It's not a bad flick, I guess.

Ten minutes later, Annabel comes waltzing into the living room, Beast behind her. I didn't even hear anyone at the door. She stops in the doorway. "Are you guys seriously watching this?"

"Shhh, this is a good part," Jude says.

She bursts into laughter and squeezes onto the couch between us.

"It was only a matter of time before you got sucked into these things." Annabel turns to me and gestures at the screen. "It's totally your kind of thing."

"What do you mean?"

"You're a hopeless romantic. Plus it's clear all men are naturally attracted to movies that subjugate women and make us look like pathetic losers who need a big strong man to take care of us."

Jude interjects. "What if men need the women just as much as they need us? There's nothing wrong with wanting companionship. Why does hopeless have to be combined with romantic? I would call it hopeful, rather. Wouldn't you?"

Annabel snorts. "No. I would call it bullshit. All this happily ever after is a bunch of hogwash and you know it."

"So, you're a cynic."

"I'm a realist."

Jude leans back, resting one arm behind Annabel on the couch. "What's wrong with believing in love?

"I believe in love, just not romantic love."

"False. What about penguins?"

She frowns. "What about them?"

"They mate for life and bring each other an engagement pebble to show their love."

"False." She throws his word back at him. "All penguins gather pebbles to build their nest. It's survival, not love. You shouldn't believe every meme you read on the internet." She flicks her fingers at the screen. "The truth is it's all about procreation and has nothing to do with some kind of world-altering romance. That's what they want you to believe."

"Who are *they*?" I ask.

"The people who make Valentine's Day candy and greeting cards and jewelry and flowers, the same people who make these movies and take your money, that's who."

"Those are legit businesses. Capitalist ventures I can get behind," Jude says.

Annabel opens her mouth, probably to issue some kind of mouthy retort, but then Reese emerges from down the hallway, rubbing her eyes.

"What's all the yelling about?" Her hair is a messy bun on the top of her head, strands escaping to form a haphazard halo around her face. She's wearing sleep shorts that barely graze midthigh and a thin camisole with narrow straps and . . . I've never seen so much of her flesh.

And I'm staring.

I rip my gaze away and turn to Annabel.

My sister. Who's sitting right next to me. She's the biggest boner killer in the room.

Beast is hulking in the recliner.

Maybe second biggest.

"How do you feel about romance?" Annabel asks Reese, pulling my attention back.

"With you?" Reese's brow creases in confusion. It's an adorable, sleepy gesture and something in my stomach flips in awareness.

Did I think adorable? About Reese? Sleep deprivation is doing funny things to my brain.

"Not me," Annabel clarifies. "Romance in general."

Reese considers it. "I'm not diametrically opposed."

"There you go." Annabel waves a hand at Reese.

"That doesn't prove anything," Jude says. "Lady, you're crazier than a soup sandwich."

"I am not."

"She's not crazy." Reese stretches and I try to ignore the sliver of stomach revealed when her shirt rides up.

Annabel hits me on the back of the head.

Clearly, I failed.

"How do you know she's not nuttier than a fruitcake?" Jude asks.

"Based on contextual cues, I believe you're using the term *crazy* to describe someone mentally deranged, which does not describe Annabel, who is obviously of sound mind. However, if you're saying she is intensely enthusiastic, or passionate about a topic—like saying someone is crazy about baseball—then you may be correct."

I'm momentarily stunned. Along with everyone else in the room.

"Huh," Jude says. "I don't have anything to say about that."

Annabel laughs. "That's right, dickweeds."

Beast seems to take some kind of offense to her comment. He stands and lumbers out of the room.

Jude claps once, loudly. "Okay then. Get ready, babies. All the fun starts in less than an hour."

A CROWD HAS GATHERED BY THE TIME WE MAKE OUR WAY to the library steps. We had to walk through the busy quad to get here, already full of giant inflatable obstacle courses, booths with information, and carts selling carnival-type food. There's a mock football game where all the players are dressed up in drag—wigs, heels, and all—to raise money for their charities, a kissing booth where you can pay for a sloppy lick from a baby pig, and a variety of other money-raising venues.

Right at ten o'clock, Jude busts out his megaphone.

"Today's Bedlam event is perhaps the most challenging yet. Let me welcome all of you to the Begonia Day scavenger hunt!"

The assembled crowd claps and whoops.

"Our competitors will be given a list of items to retrieve along with a few tasks which must be documented photographically. They have exactly two hours to meet back here. Whoever has completed the most tasks will be our day-three winner."

Beast hands Reese and me each a single sheet of paper, and my eyes run down the seven items on the list. Most of them are fairly easy.

Have a thumb war with a cop.

Prove a well-known mathematical theorem on a chalkboard.

Obtain a coin of any denomination from 1998.

Locate ten things that are red.

Take a selfie with one of the deans.

The final two tasks on the list are a little tougher.

Get a pic while wearing an official Fighting Boars Football jersey from a member of the starting lineup for today's game.

I'll have to either find a player somewhere around here—not necessarily a challenge on its own—then ask them to, what, borrow their jersey for a minute? It's either that or sneak into the locker room. I'm not sure any giant jocks will be amenable to some dude asking for their shirt, so option two might be the best shot.

And the final task: *Get a picture of Begonia in a dress.* I'm not sure how easy it will be to dress a pig, but it can't be too hard, right? I just have to find a dress . . .

No time for dwelling.

Jude does his countdown and then we're off. I run after Reese into the quad, but within moments she's disappeared into the crowd.

Might as well get the easy stuff out of the way. I find campus security first, monitoring the perimeter. There's a man and woman combo and I convince her to take the video with my phone while her partner and I engage in a thumb war.

I find a member of the track team working one of the booths, and they let me rifle through their money box until I find a coin from 1998 and switch it out with one of mine from my pocket.

While I'm there, the dean of liberal arts shows up and we take a selfie.

All the while, I take pictures of anything and everything red. Someone's shirt, a woman in red sunglasses, the fire hydrant, and a cowboy with a red handkerchief around his neck.

At one point I spot Reese across the quad with the same cops I talked to before. Annabel is with her, taking the video.

Why is my sister helping my opponent?

I shake off the thread of annoyance. Focus. Once I've gotten my ten red objects, it's time to get down to the more difficult tasks.

I'm not the best at math, but I bet I can find a theorem already written up in the math building.

On the way in, I run into Reese and Annabel on their way out.

"Hello, brother dear. Running behind, are we?"

"Hardly." I race past them and almost immediately spot a whiteboard with a formula on it. Doesn't look simple to me, but it will have to do.

Within a minute, I'm heading back out the door.

Annabel and Reese are still hovering by the entrance.

Annabel is talking. Naturally. Bossing Reese around, more like.

"Okay, now we need to get a pic in a jersey from one of those guys out at the dunking booth." Annabel points over at the group of jocks. "You should ask number thirty-four. He looks nice."

"I can't ask a guy to wear his jersey."

"Of course you can. Use your feminine wiles."

Reese is already turning red just at the thought of it. "I don't have those. And if I did, I wouldn't know what to do with them."

Annabel purses her lips, then reaches forward and, with a flick of her wrist, unsnaps the top three buttons of Reese's shirt. "Now you do. Every man's kryptonite. Boobs."

Irritation pulses through me, and it's not because Reese's cleavage is now on display. "Some of us are capable of higher thinking."

Annabel turns at the sound of my voice and shrugs. "Not many. You're a unicorn, Fitzy."

"This isn't going to work," Reese says.

"He's a boy, it will work. Now go get 'em, tiger." She smacks Reese on the bottom, making her jump and toss a surprised glance back at us.

I stop next to my sister and we watch as Reese crosses the quad on timid feet and then attempts to inject herself into their conversation. I can see the red flush creeping up her neck from a hundred yards away.

"Now, you can't be helping her. It's not fair."

She rolls her eyes, a move she's been perfecting since she was thirteen. "I do what I want. Besides, it's not like I'm actually doing the tasks, I'm just here for emotional support. Like a service dog. Now shut it, Fitz. Don't you have other things you should be doing?"

I do, but I'm distracted by the train wreck that is Reese Jackson. One of the players has finally noticed her. Reese is talking, gesticulating widely, and suddenly the brawny football player—who I think is a linebacker—reels back and guffaws. Then he's whipping his jersey over his head.

"Shit."

Annabel laughs. "She's so adorably ridorkulous. Don't you think?"

I should leave, but instead I continue to watch in a fascinated stupor while Reese gets a selfie with the jock. Then he takes her phone, still talking to her, and keys something into it. She's nodding as he hands her the phone back. Did he ask for her number?

She does have a bit of awkward charm. The half-unbuttoned shirt probably helps.

Something squirms in my stomach. I am not jealous. Not of that, anyway. Maybe it's only because she got the jersey so easily and I'm probably going to have to commit some kind of felony. I can't imagine one of the giant athletes taking off their clothes for *me*.

"Better hurry." Annabel smirks.

"It's still not fair," I can't help but grumble.

"Number forty-two is gay."

My gaze snaps to her. "Now you're helping me?"

"So you can't whine about me going along with Reese. And we're totally kicking your ass already so I figured I'd give you a fighting chance." She shrugs. "Makes it more interesting. Maybe we'll see you over at

Begonia's pen. Good luck!" She slaps me on the back and runs after Reese, who is already heading in the direction of the barn where the mascot lives.

I better get moving.

8

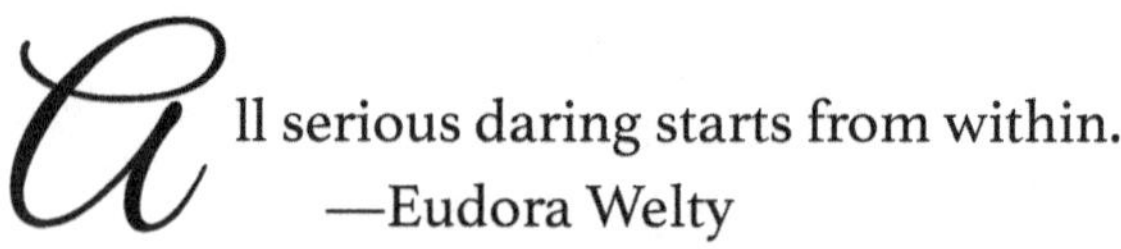

All serious daring starts from within.
—Eudora Welty

Reese

"Why do they have security for a pig?" It seems a bit much.

In a fenced-in pen outside a big red barn, Begonia rummages, snorting and chuffing. She's not a boar. But she is a giant pig. A Large White, if I had to classify her particular breed of swine. They are large, to say the least. Males can exceed eight hundred pounds.

Annabel and I are hiding around the corner of the student union building. We've already scoped out the area and procured a dress from the theater department —a red-sequined thing that will in no way shape or form ever fit on a Large White pig—and now we're trying to figure out a way to get to the mascot.

A guy looms outside the fence, wearing a Fighting Boars polo shirt and jeans. He looks like he could be the president of the student body, all proper and put together, hair slicked back and badge hanging around his neck on a Blue Falls lanyard. His arms are crossed over his chest as he scans the area and occasionally glances back at Begonia.

He clearly takes his job seriously, not even poking around on his cell phone like any other normal college kid would be doing.

"That guy is hardly what I would call intimidating. It's just a precaution because of what happened before."

"What happened before?"

Annabel eyes me with no small amount of shock. "You haven't heard about the time the mascot got murdered?"

"What?" I can't have heard her correctly.

"It's the whole reason we have Begonia Day. Reese, how can you be so smart and so clueless at the same time? It's a campus legend."

"I didn't go to freshman orientation." I didn't want to talk to people. If I don't speak, I can't stick my foot in my mouth or expose myself as the weirdo I am. I've talked to more people in the past few days than I have since I started here, I think. Probably more than any other week in my whole life.

Annabel rolls her eyes. "But everyone knows."

At my blank look she sighs, keeping her voice quiet

so it doesn't carry. "Back in the forties or something, when another team was here visiting for a game, the handler of the mascot from the Ohio Laughing Colts got too close and the horse trampled Begonia, killing her instantly. That's when Begonia Day started. Why else did you think they have Begonia Day every year?"

I shrug. "I never gave it much thought, I guess. I didn't come to the festivities last year. I . . . haven't done much socializing since college started."

"Clearly."

"How do we get around security?"

Annabel smiles. "You leave it to me."

"What are you going to do?"

"Run distraction."

"Isn't this cheating? You've probably helped me too much as it is."

She peeks around the corner one more time, then turns back to me. "Jude didn't say anything about someone assisting. And if Fitz gets here within the next ten minutes, he'll benefit too. We don't have time to argue. It's eleven thirty. We have thirty minutes. Less if you keep talking."

And with that, she leaves me behind and strides toward the guard, confidence swinging in every step of her cowboy boots.

"Hey," she says. "I'm here to take over for the next shift."

His brow furrows. "That's not for another hour."

Annabel props one hand on her hip. "Mr. Oakley sent me. You'll have to check with him."

Wow. She's really good. I almost believe her and I *know* she's lying.

I wouldn't be able to prevaricate so easily. I would be shaking in my boots, both literally and figuratively.

The preppy security guard pulls out his phone, keeping his eyes on Annabel and pushes some buttons.

What is her plan? How is this going to work? He's going to get Mr. Oakley on the phone and realize she's full of it.

"He's not answering, is he?" Annabel's smile is wide and confident. "He's in his office. Go on and talk to him. I'll wait here."

"Is this some kind of trick?" the security guard asks.

Annabel heaves an exaggerated sigh. "What in the world do you think I'm going to do to a pig? Let alone in the five minutes it's going to take for you to check with Mr. Oakley?"

"Do you have student ID?"

She pulls it out of her purse and shows him.

"Fine. But I'm bringing this with me."

He disappears around the corner and Annabel waves me over. "Hurry. We'll have less than ten minutes with the way he's hauling that stick up his ass."

"How did you know Mr. Oakley wouldn't answer?" I search the fence line for an opening.

"I didn't. But I do know he likes to hang out in the parking lot and tailgate by nine so he's probably already three sheets to the wind."

"Why do you have a student ID?"

"My old one. I graduated last year. Here, this is the gate."

I nod and then focus on getting to Begonia. I peek over the top of the fence. She's got her head in the trough, snuffling around. She's fairly calm at the moment. I can do this.

I finally find the latch but I can't get it open. "It must be locked." They really are serious about this pig.

"We don't have time to mess with it. Let me give you a boost."

Annabel helps boost me over the fence. It's a bit of a struggle. She gets me mostly on top and then I have to throw myself over.

I fall to the earth with a thud, startling Begonia from her happy foraging. She squeals and runs to the far corner of the yard.

"Here, piggy, piggy, piggy." I stand, wiping dust from my clothes and shaking out the dress.

I approach slowly, blocking her into the corner, but with a snort she sprints in my direction. I leap for her but she dodges at the last second and I end up facedown in the mud.

"Don't y'all know how to catch a pig?"

I sit up, wiping mud from my eyes.

Fitz is next to Annabel at the fence, his arms crossed and resting over the top of the pen, watching me with a smirk.

Ignoring him, I race for Begonia again, who skitters away and I end up running back and forth until I finally get close enough to leap onto her back and pull the dress over her head. "Take the picture!" I yell, holding on for dear life while Begonia tries to buck me off.

"Got it!" Annabel finally calls out.

I yank the dress off and fall back into the mud.

Begonia kicks her hooves into the dirt, spraying more mud at me before scurrying away.

"You've already lost, Fitzy." Annabel holds up the phone in triumph.

"I know. I still don't have the jersey either." He reaches over the fence, twists a knob, and the gate swings open.

Of course. It's just that easy.

I focus on the man striding toward Begonia, confidence swaggering in every step. "Why are you still doing this if you're going to lose?"

He shrugs. "Can't never could."

My brows lift. I've heard the expression before, one uttered by every Southerner over fifty at one point or another.

Annabel laughs. "Don't even get Fitz started. He doesn't give up on anything. Ever. Even when defeat is staring him right in the face like a giant pig."

"Well, it's true. You can only fail if you stop trying." His eyes are still focused on Begonia, who continues to trot back and forth, pacing the far end of the fence.

On nimble feet, he rushes at Begonia, but she skitters out of the way.

"But that doesn't make sense. There's no chance you'll get Begonia in the dress and a picture in a jersey sometime in the next," I glance down at my watch, "eighteen minutes. It's a logistical impossibility."

He's still focused on the pig, who is once again running back and forth along the fence line. "I don't care."

I blink. I don't understand his logic.

It's confusing and yet . . . I'm weirdly impressed.

But should I be? Isn't it a waste of effort? I would never keep going if I were in his situation.

What would it be like, to keep pushing no matter the obstacles in my way?

To have enough confidence that I wasn't afraid to fail?

"Come on outta there, Reese," Annabel calls. "Let's get back to the library." She waves an impatient hand at me.

I glance over at her and then back at Fitz. She's right. It's just a quick jaunt and I've won this round and the rights to sleeping in a quiet bed for the night.

Begonia squeals behind me and I turn in time to see Fitz tumble backward into the mud.

"I admire your dedication and perseverance," I tell Fitz.

He stands to face me and underneath the splatter of dirt on his face, his eyes are gleaming, mouth tilted in a smile. So he remembers our conversation the night before.

And before I can give it any thought, my feet carry me away from the fence and back toward Begonia.

"What are you doing?" Annabel yells. "He's the enemy."

"I'm winning either way."

Fitz is grinning at me, mud splattered all over his shirt and up his neck, and somehow he's still glowing with a natural charisma I could never replicate.

It almost makes it worth the effort I'm about to expend.

"You helped me too," Fitz tells Annabel.

"I gave you intel, which clearly did no good. I was evening the odds, not doing the actual task for you."

"Ready?" I crowd Begonia on one side while Fitz approaches her from the front. I throw myself at the pig, catching her back hooves with my hands, lying facedown in the dirt while Fitz gets the dress over her squirming head.

"You're both crazy," Annabel shouts. "And stupid."

"Can we do the name calling another time? I have a pig to dress up here," Fitz says.

I can't see much from my position on the ground, but I hear some shuffling and squirming, then Fitz yells, "Got it!"

I release Begonia, and she scurries over to the shade by her trough.

I roll onto my butt and find Fitz hovering in front of me, his hand held out.

After a moment's hesitation, I reach up and he grasps my hand, pulling me to my feet. I try to ignore the electric shock that shoots into my palm when our hands meet. It's nothing. Just a static charge or something.

"Do you think she's been traumatized?" I wipe my muddy hands on my muddier pants.

"I think I am. You smell something awful." He grins.

"You're not much better."

We're both covered in gunk. My clothes are ruined. "But that was fun, right?" he asks.

I scrunch my face. "Is fun the word we want to use here?"

He laughs. "Come on, champ." He holds the gate open for me, happy even in defeat, which surprises me again. What happened to the rude jerk from a couple days ago? Is this all a ruse? Maybe he does have the jersey pic and I unwittingly aided him in victory.

But no, we jog back to the library, where Jude is holding court and I'm declared the event winner, handed the key, and subjected to both applause from those who bet on me and groans of dismay from those who bet on Fitz.

It's now two to one, in my favor.

I don't see Fitz in the crowd anywhere. He must've already left.

And I've won.

So why do I feel guilty?

Football is to Texas as backbones are to vertebrates. The entire state would collapse into a bloody heap without it.

I thought partying at Jude's during the week was chaos, but it being a Saturday night after Begonia Day, combined with a Fighting Boars football victory, tonight's chaos makes previous evenings seem like teatime at an old folks' home.

After slinking around the house and observing the line of people stretching out the door, I still can't believe it. Tonight, everyone has to pay five dollars to get in the door, but even that isn't a deterrent.

Almost the whole crowd is dressed up in Begonia shirts or pig masks or pig noses or all three.

There are so many kegs in the backyard, the gleaming silver is probably visible from space. There's also a DJ lording over a dance floor in the grass where the chutes and ladders game once resided.

Annabel disappeared after the scavenger hunt and Fitz is here somewhere, socializing. Beast is managing the line out front, and lord only knows where Jude is.

Despite the fact I know no one, everyone is kind . . . and overly familiar. Which I still can't get used to. Random strangers clap me on the back, offering congratulations or saying hi and asking me questions about my parents, but it's too much.

The house is packed, barely any room to breathe. Before the party even really gets going, I manage an escape, hiding in the room with the door safely locked, shut in like the recluse I am. Thank God I won today.

I try to get some schoolwork done, but it isn't easy with a backdrop of pounding bass. After an hour, I'm not focusing on anything but the noise, and I have to pee so bad my back teeth are floating. Can't avoid the necessary any longer.

I make a quick escape, locking the door behind me and pulling the key over my head.

And of course, there's a line to the bathroom at the front of the house and another at the one Fitz and I share.

After waiting for what feels like hours but is probably less than ten minutes, I emerge refreshed. However, my relief doesn't last long.

There's a couple in front of the bedroom door.

Not only in front of it, but barring all possible entry.

He's got her back against the door. She's moaning and throwing her head back.

Now he's kissing her neck and . . . What do I do? Should I say something? Oh dear, her legs are wrapped around his waist and he's . . . I'm burning with embarrassment, but no one else is paying much attention to the live-action porno against my door.

How can they be doing that in public, where anyone and everyone can see? Although, Abby did much the same while we resided in the dorms together. But I was at least sleeping. Or trying to. And it was just me, not a whole line of people waiting for a bathroom at a party.

Now what? I suppose I can wait them out. If my recollection of Abby's various paramours is any kind of indicator, they'll be finished in fifteen minutes or less.

I weave through the mess of people in the hall through the living room and finally out into the backyard, where I can breathe and the stench of deodorant, cologne, and beer isn't quite so prevalent.

Making my way to the edge of the yard, I stop near a hedge where it's dark and I can observe without being spotted.

People are dancing, shouting, laughing, drinking. Some guy does a keg stand, much to the delight of the onlookers, and then when he is deposited back on his feet, he immediately turns over and pukes.

I guess this is fun?

Fitz is talking to some guys in one corner of the yard. I watch him for a few minutes, remembering our brief accord earlier today.

He's laughing with some other guys, enjoying himself. He no longer has that kicked-puppy look like he did immediately after the whole Abby thing. As a matter of fact, he's seemed okay the past couple of days, except for the conversation I overheard with his momma. Is everything okay with his dad? Has he told his parents about Abby yet?

Not that it's any of my business.

And then as if I've conjured her with my thoughts, Abby spills out from the house onto the back patio.

She looks . . . trashed.

Horrified fascination fills me as she stumbles into people, nearly yanking them down in an attempt to remain upright.

I want to hate her. I should hate her. She was terrible to me, and living with her was as easy as pissing up a rope. But seeing her here, now, like this? I feel nothing but pity.

She grabs on to a guy dancing near the DJ and yells, like she's trying to get the attention of everyone in the yard.

Then like a switch has been flipped, her glassy-eyed glaze turns into a laser the exact moment she spots Fitz. The laughter abruptly ceases and her lip wobbles and her eyes fill.

Her mouth forms his name.

Then she's stumbling in his direction.

9

Close the door on the past. You don't try to forget the mistakes, but you don't dwell on it. You don't let it have any of your energy, or any of your time, or any of your space.

—Johnny Cash

Fitz

When Reese steps into the backyard, I'm almost immediately aware of her presence, despite the fact that there have got to be a hundred people milling around between us, and that's just in the backyard.

Maybe it's because she's not like anyone else. She's not dressed up, not calling attention to herself. She's just wearing a plain blue T-shirt and jeans. She's so clearly not trying to impress anyone.

In fact, it's more like she wants to hide.

As I'm having that exact thought, she scurries like a rabbit into the dark shadows by the fence line and I try not to laugh, forcing myself to pay attention to the conversation with some guys from track.

It's hard. I want to see what she's going to do next.

My focus is split between the discussion and keeping tabs on Reese, so I don't notice Abby until she's latched on to my arm like a piranha.

"Fitz? Baby?" The words are slurred, her eyes glazed.

Immediately, I twist away, attempting to extricate my arm from her grasp without drawing too much attention.

"Now isn't a great time." I keep my voice low, which means I have to lean closer to her while also trying to pull away.

Never would be a great time.

"I really miss you." Her eyes fill with tears and she stumbles into me, forcing my arm around her to keep us both upright.

I'm stuck like a duck in a dry pond.

Trying to keep my cursing on the inside, I offer an apologetic smile to the guys and pull Abby to the side of the yard, as far as we can get from the thumping bass and music and crowd.

"What do you want, Abby?"

"I want to talk."

"Okay." I cross my arms over my chest. "Talk."

Her mouth opens and she flails like a fish for a few seconds before I help her out.

"We're over. There isn't anything to talk about."

"Fitz, you're my best friend."

"Friends don't treat each other the way you've been treating me."

"But that's the thing. Friends aren't always sweethearts and it's like we shouldn't have done what we did but it's my fault for always needing . . . needing something. I don't remember." She laughs, but the sound isn't happy. It has sharp edges, hysteria threaded through the middle.

"What are you talking about? I tried to be your friend, Abby. You tried to manipulate me for . . . I don't know, some kind of sick amusement?"

She winces. "You make it sound so cruel."

"It was cruel!" And now I'm yelling. I stop and take a deep breath. "I can't do this." I start to walk away but Abby grabs my hand.

"Fitz, please. We need to talk."

"Maybe when you're sober."

I pull my hand away and get a lucky break when one of Abby's friends comes over to talk to her. Grabbing a play from one of Reese's books, I hide behind the nearest bush, stepping between the hedges and into the shadows.

And of course, only a few feet away is Reese herself. I swear she was on the other side of the yard before. She must've been circling the perimeter.

"Hey," I say.

"Hey."

"What are you doing hiding in the bushes again? I figured you'd be luxuriating in your win. You know you can hide behind the locked door. No foliage needed."

I think she laughs a little, but it's too dark to see her face. "I was but . . ."

"But what?"

"I had to use the bathroom and when I came back, uh, there was . . ."

I groan. "Don't tell me someone was doing it on the bed in there. Didn't you lock it?"

"I did lock it. It's not that. They weren't inside the room, they were up against . . . They were," her hands flitter like clumsy birds in the dim light, "using the door."

A startled laugh escapes me. "And you couldn't tell them to move?"

I can't see her skin turn pink in the darkness of the yard, but I can imagine it, having witnessed her blush at least ten times an hour over the past few days.

"Fitz!" The call rings out too close for comfort. Abby is stumbling this way, one of her friends trailing behind her.

"Goddammit," I mutter under my breath as Reese watches the scene intently. "Got any ideas?"

"Yes. Come on." Reese shocks me to hell by grabbing my hand and tugging me along the fence line, around the corner of the house, through a side door that leads into the garage and finally back into the house.

Once we're in the hallway, she drops my hand. "You're welcome."

I use my suddenly cold hand to rub the back of my neck. "Thanks. And while we're here." I stalk past her to where, yes, there is a couple making out enthusiastically, thumping against the door.

Thump, thump, thump.

Christ. It's like one bad flashback after another.

It makes it easy for me to walk up, pound heavily on the door right next to their heads. "Time to move on somewhere else, folks."

They must hear me, though they don't stop their make-out session. Instead, Romeo hoists Juliette up higher on his hips and they slide to the wall next to the door. But at least they aren't blocking it anymore.

I bow, flourishing one hand toward the door. "Ma'am. Your humble abode awaits."

Reese darts forward with the key, pushing the door open. "Thanks," she murmurs as she passes, the word so quiet I nearly miss it with the raging party around us.

"No problem."

She starts to shut the door but then hesitates on the threshold. Only an inch of space is open, and her eyes are wide and a little uncertain.

A shriek rings out above the music, coming from the living room. "Fitz!"

My shoulders tense.

Abby.

I can't see her yet, but I don't have much time before that inevitability.

Reese's eyes meet mine, then the inch of space widens. "Escape hatch?"

Yes, please.

I step through the door and she closes it behind us,

muting the pounding music and jumble of voices. It's a whole different world in the small space, the Christmas lights casting a glow like early-morning rays of sun.

I sit on the corner of the bed and brace my elbows on my knees. "Sorry I'm ruining your night to have the room to yourself. She'll eventually pass out or her friends will drag her off soon enough, then I'll leave you to it."

"It's fine."

So she says, but she's still standing by the door, arms crossed over her chest, looking everywhere but at me.

When she finally speaks, her voice is tentative. "Are you . . . Never mind."

"What is it?"

"It's none of my business." She uncrosses her arms, then crosses them again.

"Go ahead and ask. If I don't want to answer, I won't."

Her chin lifts in a move I'm coming to recognize as the one she uses when she's getting stubborn. "Are you gonna get back together with her?"

"If I were, do you think I'd be itching to run away?"

She shrugs. "People always do things that don't make sense when it comes to relationships."

"I guess that's true but the answer is no. No, I'm not going to get back together with her. I don't think there's anything she could do to change my mind. It will be a struggle to stay friends." The words roll off my tongue with surprising ease, startling me with the fact that they taste like truth.

Even though we've been over as a couple for a

month, I always thought she would be there, in some part of my life, because she always has been.

Maybe she will be a friend again, but right now, that future looks hazy at best.

Reese sits on the bed near the pillow, as far from me as she can get. "You guys were together a long time." The words are soft, tentative.

"Too long, maybe." I laugh without humor.

"It's a big change."

"It is," I agree. "But at the same time, it's not. Not really. Things between Abby and me . . . they've been changing for a while. I didn't want to accept it at first. I was living in la-la land and she was living in . . . well, anywhere-but-with-me land, that's for sure. I hate to say Annabel was right, but she's been telling me for longer than I care to mention to cut Abby loose."

"Annabel doesn't believe in romance in general though."

"This is very true."

"And you do?"

I shrug. "My parents have been together since they were both knee high to a grasshopper, over twenty years."

"That's sweet."

"They have this epic love story. So do my grandparents. They were married for sixty years, had a load of kids together, always acted like newlyweds, the whole nine yards. I always thought I would have the same thing."

We're silent for a few seconds while the rest of the

house pulses in energetic revelry. "If your family is full of great relationships, then why does Annabel have such negative views on love and romance?"

"I have no idea. She's always been a pessimist about that stuff, or as she likes to say, a realist."

She nods and sits back a little on the bed, her tense shoulders relaxing a smidge. "My parents have a grand romance too. I can see why Annabel might see it as a detriment."

"Why's that?"

"Because they put their own desires above all else."

"What do you mean?"

"It's difficult to explain." She bites her lip, considering me for a second before continuing. "My parents are artists."

I nod. "The Jacksons. Everyone knows about them. Most famous people in town, with the exception of ol' Roy."

"Right. They met at a show in New York City when they were in their twenties. They connected immediately. Got married within weeks of meeting each other. They're both very passionate people. Passionate about their art and about each other—to the exclusion of everyone and everything else, including their children. I barely saw them growing up. Granny came to live with us after Grandpappy died, when I was ten. Before that, my older sister, Scarlett, basically raised me."

"Scarlett Jackson? I think I've heard of her. She's a chef or something, right?" I settle back on the bed, following her lead so I can lean against the wall and stretch my legs out. I remember Momma telling me about some rumors involving Scarlett and Bruce Conway, a local businessman. A local *married* businessman. Not sure exactly what happened there, but Scarlett left town shortly after the rumors started. In a town as small as this, you can't sneeze sideways without some detail of it getting around.

"Yep. An amazing one. She moved to New York City last year, chasing her dreams. She's starting her own business, mingling with celebrities, the whole thing."

A shout outside the door startles her into her formerly tense posture.

I ignore the noise and gesture for her to continue.

"Anyway, I guess my point is that they are happy, but it had a price. For Scarlett and me, anyway."

"What price?"

She fidgets with the edge of her T-shirt, not meeting my eyes. "The price of being normal."

"What do you mean? You are normal."

She laughs and watches me out of the corner of her eyes. "Says the man who no less than five days ago thought I had special needs."

Heat fills my face along with a healthy dose of shame. "I never said that. And I was an ass."

"I won't argue with you."

"I've been proven wrong, Reese. It's not an excuse, but I was in a bad place and wanting to lash out at someone. You happened to be convenient. I know better now. You're smart. Like, really smart."

Now it's her turn to flush and look away. "I'm above average maybe, but so are a lot of people."

"You're being modest. I've seen your physics book. And you killed me at trivia. Wait. The math problem, during the scavenger hunt. Did you write it?"

Her head ducks. "Yes."

"That was not a simple theorem."

"It was for me."

She won't look at me. My eyes trace over her jawline, her lips curved in a bow, her hands clasped in her lap, and a tendril of attraction wraps around me, along with a whisper of intimidation. "You're lucky. I wish I were so smart." Maybe then I could graduate early and help my parents that much sooner.

"Except I can't even decide on a major."

"Why not?

She blinks. "It's hard to explain. I'm . . ." She glances away and then back. "I'm a polymath."

"A what now?"

"It's a person of wide-ranging knowledge or learning. Someone whose expertise spans a significant number of subject areas. The term itself is a derivative of poly, meaning many, and *manthanein,* a Greek verb meaning to learn."

I stare at her. "Reese, this is amazing."

She won't meet my eyes. Instead, she picks up the pillow and holds it in her lap, fidgeting with the fabric at the corner.

"You can literally do anything."

"But don't you see?" Her eyes meet mine, flashing in

frustration. "It's impossible to pick only one thing. Our current global economy is hyperspecialized, while I'm a student of all things but a master of none. My parents are brilliant artists. Scarlett is a brilliant chef. I am more of a jack-of-all-trades. I can't find any one specific thing I want to learn or excel at above all others."

"Huh. I still can't see this as a disadvantage. You're so smart that the sky is the limit."

"But the whole point of college and picking a career is to find that limit. Isn't it?"

"I don't know." I never thought about it that way. "I think it's more than that. It's about doing something you enjoy, something you feel passionate about."

"Passionate?" Her head tips to one side.

"You know, isolate the things that make you inordinately happy. Or even angry. Anything that excites you. You could even create a separate list for each subject, listing the pros and cons."

Her brows furrow. "I've been struggling with this for more than a year, and yet you make it sound so easy."

"It is. You're already doing the hard part."

"What do you mean?"

I shift closer to her. "That day, in the housing office, when I took the flyer and ran. You didn't give up or stay behind. You followed me. When we had to jump in the kiddie pool full of whipped cream, you were green around the gills and pale as a ghost. But you still did it."

Her mouth pops open and she's staring at me like I've sprouted three heads. But I keep talking. "You'll be okay. You'll find your path. Maybe you'll pick the wrong major, or maybe you won't. Maybe it will be the best thing you've ever done."

She blinks at me, still processing my words. "Maybe. Either way, I have to pick soon. I'm running out of time."

Her eyes are dark and there's a crease between her brows. I want to console her somehow, but I have no more words. I'm about to lay a reassuring hand over hers when Abby's shrill voice rings out over the din outside. "Where's the bathroom?"

"She's still out there." Reese's words are ominous, as if we're speaking of the grim reaper.

"Sounds like it." I heave a sigh and drop my head back against the wall. "She wasn't always like this, you know."

"I would hope so, since you stayed together for so long. But then, you wouldn't be so quick to give her up, would you? You're not one to give up on anything you set your mind to."

I smile. "My momma always says I'm stubborn as a blue-nosed mule."

She laughs. "Not me."

"Really? I wouldn't have thought so."

"I'm changeable. Or maybe . . . I'm chang*ing*."

She really is. Despite the huddling in the bushes.

A loud bang hits the door.

"Fitz! I know you're in there!"

We share a look. Abby. Again.

"I'm sorry," I mouth to Reese. I open my mouth to yell something, tell Abby to get lost or whatever but then suddenly Reese's hand is there, covering my mouth.

Our eyes meet and she shakes her head before whispering, "Better to let her think she's wrong and lose interest. If you speak, she'll dig in her heels. She wants your attention."

I blink at her and then she removes her hand from over my mouth.

We stare at each other, listening to muffled laughter and drunken talk in the background. A soothing voice is murmuring to Abby, telling her to leave with them.

Thank God.

My gaze narrows on Reese.

She was right. Abby *does* crave attention, and if she knew I was in here with Reese, she woulda been more stubborn than me.

"You know Abby almost better than I do."

She shrugs and glances away. "You learn a lot when you live with someone."

It makes me wonder exactly what her experience was, living with Abby. Did Abby ever even *mention* her roommate? I have a vague recollection of her complaining about living with a weirdo, how it sucked to bunk with a troll, but she would probably get the girl to move out.

And now I have to wonder, just how horrible *was* Abby to Reese?

I'm about to ask, but she speaks first.

"You'll find someone else. Someone better."

I chuckle without mirth. She's reassuring me when she's the one who's been treated badly. By me and by Abby. "I thank you for the compliment, but I can't imagine it. I wouldn't know what to do. I've never had any other girlfriends. It's hard to imagine being with someone else."

"I can't imagine it either."

I tilt my head. "No long-term boyfriends?"

Her laugh is quick and shocked. "No."

Wait. I laser in on her eyes. "Does that mean . . . I mean, have you ever— No, never mind, it's none of my business."

She pulls the pillow into her lap and then fidgets with the edge of the pillowcase fabric. "You've seen me. I can barely talk to people. What makes you think I could reach the point of . . . making out with someone or whatever?"

I struggle to hide my shock, schooling my features to remain impassive. *Make out?* I was thinking she's a virgin, not that she's literally never been kissed. I mean, even middle schoolers play spin the bottle. But . . . nothing? I don't know how to respond, and I definitely don't want to ask her to clarify. As a matter of fact, the knowledge she's so untouched makes her even more attractive. Undeniable heat fills my stomach.

What does that say about me? I'm a Neanderthal. This isn't the Victorian era. Humanity has progressed somewhat since the cave-man days. I think. No doubt I've become so used to Abby's poor treatment that Reese's careful approach makes her even more tempting. The whole thing is so confusing, I'm completely discombobulated and it's the only excuse for what I say next.

"You're not unattractive."

She laughs. "Wow. Thanks."

"That's not what . . . not what I meant. I think you're very pretty. When you let people see you. It's just, I don't know." I'm being a dick. Again. "It's like you prefer to be invisible."

Her brows lift. "How do you know?"

"The bushes are your favorite part of this house. I'm going to start calling you bush lady."

She laughs. "I'll ask you not to mention anything about me and my bush in the same sentence, thank you very much."

"Oh wow." A startled laugh breaks out of me and I fall back on the bed in fake shock. "You made a joke about pubes. I can't believe it. I'm dead."

She's laughing and turning red and I wonder what she would say if I offered to be her first kiss, but then I push the thought away.

Ridiculous.

Besides, we hate each other.

Don't we?

10

Life is not a spectator sport. If you're going to spend your whole life in the grandstand just watching what goes on, in my opinion you're wasting your life.

—Jackie Robinson

Reese

It's so warm and comfortable I don't want to move. Like I'm sleeping in a perfectly warm stove. Except the stove is only at my back. And around my waist.

And there's a calm wind pulsing against my neck.

No. Not wind.

Puffs of air, gentle ones. Breaths. Someone is breathing. Against my neck.

I open my eyes to a blank white wall beginning to

glow with the rays of sun filtering through the small window.

I'm at Jude's. Lying in the narrow bed. There's a wall of smooth heat at my back and an arm around my torso, tethering me in place.

A strong, lean, muscular arm.

Holy Pythagoras.

I'm *sleeping* with Fitz.

He's *spooning* me.

What do I do?

My heart accelerates in my chest like a drum beat so loud and hard he's gotta hear it. It's like a game of Jumanji is about to start in here.

Before I can decide to move or not to move, the choice is taken from me.

His phone buzzes across the hard surface of the nightstand and he immediately rolls away, taking the heat with him.

He fumbles and the phone abruptly ceases its bleating tone.

I screw my eyes shut and don't move a single muscle.

"Sorry." His whispered voice is a raspy murmur in the muted daylight.

My mouth is dry. I swallow but don't have a chance to speak.

"I have a race." The bed dips and lifts as he gets to his feet.

The dresser opens, clothes rustling, but still I don't look.

"I'm sorry I . . . I sort of took over your room on a

night you won." He's still whispering, like he wants to talk to me but isn't sure I'm awake.

Is he apologizing because he regrets falling asleep with me? Like I must be some kind of monster to sleep with or something? Maybe I stink. This whole thing is weird and awkward and exactly why I don't interact with people. What would a normal person do in this situation?

Probably not what I'm doing, which is remaining silent.

Fitz speaks again. "I'm running late but . . . ah, I'll see you later."

It's not until he's shut the door behind him that I relax.

He has to think I'm the biggest freak.

I can't believe we slept together, wrapped up like a double helix.

I've never done that with anyone. If I had more time, maybe I could have enjoyed the sensation instead of getting tense and strange and anxious.

He was so warm. I've never felt breath on the back of my neck. Never had strong arms around me, like they wanted to be there. I wish I could have hung on to the moment a little bit longer—lord knows when I'll have the opportunity again. Would it be weird to ask to cuddle?

Definitely weird. Especially since if I do get the chance again, I'll probably just make it creepy.

I roll over and attempt to fall back asleep but the

sheets smell like Fitz, deodorant, and fresh air. Homey and comfortable.

And now I'm definitely awake and not going back to sleep.

Might as well brave the rest of the house. I imagine it's a mess after last night.

But once I'm up and out, I'm surprised to find that while there are a few errant cups and pig noses left behind, it's mostly clean.

How does Jude do it?

Beast is in the kitchen. He hands me a mug full of hot coffee as soon as I enter.

"Y'all are magicians or something." I take the cup from him. "Thank you."

I move to the living room, sitting in the bay window, watching the birds chirp outside while I drink my coffee in the silence and let my thoughts tumble around.

Now that I've had a chance to talk to Fitz about Abby, I can see how hard it must have been for him to give her up, maybe not relationship-wise, but to lose a lifetime of friendship.

No wonder he kept her around for so long. Plus it seems Abby did her best to hide her true colors around Fitz. I'm surprised she got away with it as long as she did. Cheetahs can't change their stripes—as Granny always says. The truth outs always, eventually.

His will to stick is admirable, but it also means he won't give up on the room until the bitter end. My stomach sinks. One of us will have to leave when the games are over. It's not going to be easy to beat Fitz, but I'm not gonna give up either.

While the house is still quiet, I call Granny.

"Yep," she answers.

"Hey, it's me."

"Tootsie Roll, you comin' over for supper?"

"It is Sunday. Why wouldn't I be there?" I haven't ever missed a Sunday supper at home. It's tradition.

"I thought you might have a bee in your bonnet over the whole gun thing."

"No. It's fine. I might bring a friend too." Annabel wanted to hang out later, but maybe I can get her to come to dinner.

"Well, that's all right then. You bring as many friends as you like."

We hang up and I get back to my coffee and thinking about my conversation with Fitz last night.

What do I want to do? What makes me feel . . . excited?

I grab a notebook from my bag and sit back down and make a list, like he suggested.

Number one is easy. I definitely want to do something where I can continue to learn new things. But beyond that . . . I bite my lip and doodle in the margins. I like math. I write it down. Science. History. Literature. Writing. Oh, dear this is getting too long. And how can I possibly put them in any kind of sequential order?

I'm still sitting there, thinking, when Annabel comes into the living room from somewhere down the hall.

"Oh. Hey, Reese."

She's wearing a T-shirt and boxers covered in . . . is that Mr. Bojangles?

"Hey, Annabel."

"Whatcha doing?" She sits next to me and picks up my coffee from the windowsill, helping herself to a long swallow.

"I *was* enjoying some coffee."

"It's good." She lifts it in cheers before taking another drink. "What's the list about?"

I hold the notebook to my chest. "I'll tell you if you explain to me why you're wearing Jude's boxers."

She puts the mug down and spreads her hands. "There's no story here. I just needed something to sleep in, you know."

Jude appears in the doorway. "Did you want some coffee?" he asks her.

"I had some."

He's smiling, and she's staring back at him but I can't see her expression since she's turned away.

No one speaks for a few long seconds and then Annabel stands abruptly. "I gotta get going." She takes off back down the hall.

Jude shrugs and heads back to the kitchen, yelling, "Mornin', Reese," over his shoulder.

Huh.

Within minutes, Annabel is back, fully dressed, purse in hand.

"We still hanging out later?" I call when she races past the open doorway.

"Um." She appears back in the doorway, her eyes

darting toward the kitchen, where Jude is whistling along to the sounds of coffee brewing. “Yeah, sure.”

“Wanna go to supper at Granny’s?”

“Sounds good.”

“Gotta be there right at five. Meet back here at four thirty?”

Jude’s whistling gets a little louder.

“That’s fine. Good. Great. See you.” Then she disappears so fast, I think an Annabel-shaped outline forms midair.

Well, isn’t that interesting.

11

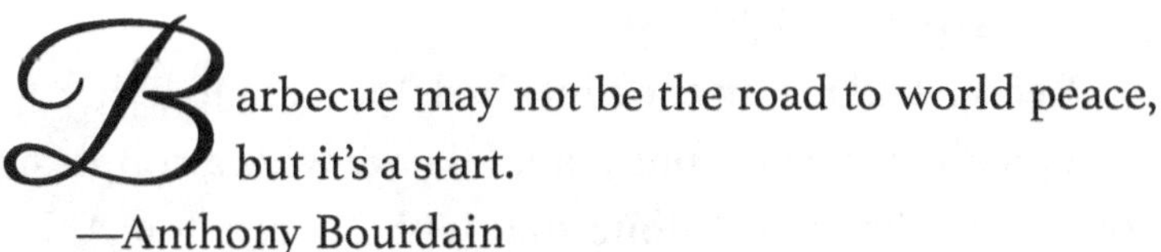

Barbecue may not be the road to world peace, but it's a start.

—Anthony Bourdain

Fitz

"How was the meet?" Jude asks as soon as I walk into the kitchen.

I glance over at the dining table, where all my housemates are sitting. "Fine." I head to the sink, filling up a cup and chugging it down.

I placed third in the 2400 and we got second in the relay, but I spent the rest of the time trying to avoid Abby, who did worse than ever, coming in last or close to it for every event.

That's what happens when you party too hard and can't put in your best effort. Or any effort at all, really.

Now I'm dusty and dirty and need to hit the shower. "House meeting?"

"Nah, just doing some numbers," Jude says.

Beast has his notebook open and Reese is sitting next to him, close enough to read whatever he's got in there.

Weird.

Escaping to the room to grab clean clothes, I give only a fleeting glance to the bed where we slept together last night.

We slept last night.

Reese. And me. In the same bed. We slept together.

I mean, not really, but yeah. Like we were a couple or something. I've never done that with anyone but Abby, ever. And even with Abby it didn't happen more than a handful of times.

And then I had to bail out for the meet and now I feel like a bit of a schmuck for it, even though we didn't actually do anything and even though she tried to pretend she was sleeping. No one can be that tense while they sleep.

I hope it doesn't make things tense between us again. I don't think it will. It's a physical attraction. That's all.

I shower quickly and head back to the kitchen for a snack. It's Jude's night to cook and I'm liable to eat an entire horse.

"What's for dinner?" I open the fridge for a snack.

"I don't know yet, but you have to see this," Jude says.

I walk over to the table and Jude points out a column

of numbers on the notebook in front of Reese. "Do this one. Show him."

We lock gazes, her dark blue irises lighter in the bright daylight streaming in through the kitchen windows, but then she jerks her eyes away.

She nods at Jude and then focuses down the page.

Jude holds up the calculator from his lap as Reese recites the number.

"Four thousand seven hundred and eighty-five point one two."

Jude lowers the calculator. His voice is awestruck. "You're a genius."

"I'm not. Not really." Her cheeks are pink. "More like a circus freak."

"Never that," Jude says before I can say something similar. "Babies, you are amazing."

Her flush deepens.

A knock at the front has everyone turning. Annabel's voice calls out, "Reese?"

"Come on in," Jude says.

"Why are you always here?" I ask when she walks into the kitchen.

"Aw, I love it when you talk sweet to me, brother mine." She stops next to me and gives me a quick kiss on the cheek. "I'm here to pick up Reese."

"Where you guys going?" Jude asks.

"Supper at the Jackson ranch," Annabel answers.

"Granny's making barbeque," Reese adds.

Jude rubs his stomach. "I've a hankering for some homemade biscuits."

"Sorry, Van Wilder, but you haven't been invited to sample Granny's smoked brisket."

"But wouldn't you know it, barbeque is my favorite food. And I reckon it's not up to you whether I'm invited or not."

"Buy your own food."

"What can I say, darlin', poor boys got poor ways."

"Except you're not poor." Annabel's eyes narrow and Jude's unflappable smile falters for a brief second.

"You can come," Reese speaks into the silence.

Jude grins slowly, his eyes never leaving Annabel, who huffs in annoyance.

"You can all come. Granny always cooks enough food to get the whole county full as a tick."

"Shotgun!" Jude yells, standing up and making for the door. "Beast, you coming?"

Beast lumbers after Jude, tucking the notebook into his jacket.

"Reese has shotgun since it's her house we're going to." Annabel follows them out the door.

"Did you want to come along?" Reese asks, her expression neutral.

I'm half starved. I want to go with them. But at the same time, I don't know if spending more time with Reese is a good idea.

She's . . . I don't know. I don't know how to sort out the emotions pressing at me. I remember waking up with her in my arms, soft, sweet. How she helped me with the pig. How she could have gone off about what a bitch Abby was to her, but held it back.

I'm not ready to jump into anything new. And Reese and I are competing. There are a million reasons this is the worst idea ever, and yet the little head below my waist is panting like a shaggy dog in a July heat wave.

"No. I'm good." My stomach growls and I whirl away, hoping she can't hear it even though to me it sounds like a rumble from the earth itself.

"Okay. See you later."

I nod, ignoring the twinge of disappointment when the front door slams shut.

What did I want, for her to insist that I come along?

Maybe I sort of did.

I watch from the kitchen window while they try and sort themselves inside Annabel's car, an old two-door Honda Civic hand-me-down from Momma. Not a large vehicle by any means, and that fact is proven as Beast tries to tuck his large frame into the miniscule back seat.

I chuckle as Jude attempts to climb in through the back window. Annabel is yelling at both of them, her face turning red while her mouth flaps.

Reese stands to the side, watching and laughing.

My gaze is drawn to her, her smile, the light in her eyes, and then I notice movement behind her, down the street.

A lone figure walks toward the house, arms wrapped around herself, blonde hair, a pink sweater that I instantly recognize.

Abby. Heading this way.

Oh, hell no.

Forgetting all my worries about the swiftly growing attraction to Reese, I hurry out the door.

"Wait, I'm coming." I lock the door behind me.

"Of course you are." Jude's finally levered himself into the back seat next to Beast.

"There's no room," Annabel says. "Drive your own car."

"But it's parked two blocks over." All the street spots were taken when I got home. I glance down the road. Abby's getting closer. "And it's full of boxes."

"You can sit on Beast's lap," Jude suggests.

"You sit on his lap," I say.

"Nope." Jude's smile is knowing as his eyes dart down the street.

Jude's gonna win this game of chicken, and he knows it.

"Where's Reese's car?" I make one last-ditch attempt.

"Parked outside the Spellman Science Center," she says.

Which is like a mile away.

"Fine," I relent, getting in on the driver's side and angling awkwardly, half off and half on Beast's lap.

My head is hitting the roof of the small car and my knees are jammed up against the seat, but I don't care.

"Sorry, big guy," I tell Beast.

He, of course, says nothing.

Once everyone is situated, Reese slides into the front seat and Annabel starts the car.

"Well look if it isn't Tramparella," Annabel says as we

pass Abby on the road. "No wonder you wanted to high-tail it out of there."

"How far is your house?" I ask Reese, changing the subject.

"About ten minutes."

We drive down Main Street, passing the Frostee Freeze where I took Abby for our first date, then ol' Roy, who waves and laughs at our packed clown car.

It's a long ten minutes until we're pulling down a dusty gravel drive.

When Annabel parks, I don't see much until I've maneuvered myself out of the back seat. I stretch my stiff legs and glance around.

It's a ranch-style home with a large wooden porch, all done up in random colors that should look odd on a house but somehow work. It looks exactly like somewhere I would picture Reese living, slightly bizarre and yet somehow perfectly put together.

The property is large, its tree line stretching as far as the eye can see. There are no other homes in sight. A small garden sits off to the side, surrounded by a low fence. A lone sprinkler spits water in a rhythmic circle, the sound reminiscent of hot August days and late-night cookouts.

"Why aren't you living here?" Annabel asks.

I scuff a bit of gravel with a foot. "Yeah. That would solve a lot of problems."

We follow Reese up the drive to the porch. "Granny wouldn't let me."

"Why not?" I ask.

She bites her bottom lip. "When I tried to come back, she pulled a shotgun on me."

Jude rubs his hands together. "I have a good feeling about this dinner."

I frown at the colorful structure, pushing my brows together. "She's not gonna try and shoot us, is she?"

"Just don't do anything to piss her off."

"What kinda stuff pisses her off?"

"Rabbits eating her vegetable garden, liars and cheats, people who don't like her cooking, and Californians."

Jude nods once. "Duly noted."

"Are your parents home?" Annabel asks as we file up to the front door.

"No. They're off traveling somewhere in Europe. It's only Granny right now."

Reese opens the door and calls out. "Granny? I brought some friends over for dinner."

Granny calls from the rear of the house, "I'm out back."

The smell of charcoal and meat wafts in the air as we walk through an open entry with high ceilings and dark wooden floors. Reese leads us through a doorway into a living area. The walls are covered with a variety of paintings and murals in vibrant colors, every available surface featuring statues and odd little artifacts and trinkets.

Out through a set of french doors, we find Granny sitting next to the smoker, puffing on a pipe. She's in overalls and a cowboy hat, her grey hair lying in two long braids down her back. No bubbles in *her* pipe. From the smell wafting about the area, I'm about ninety-eight percent certain she's got marijuana in it.

"Who've we got here now?" She sets her pipe on the arm of the bright-blue chair.

"This is Annabel." Reese points her out and then motions to me. "Her brother, Fitz."

"And who's this big hunky fella?" She stands and eyes Beast up and down.

"This is . . . Beast."

"He sure is."

My, what big teeth you have, Granny.

"I'm Jude Parker." Jude extends a hand. "It's a pleasure to meet you, ma'am."

She shakes Jude's hand with clear strength.

"I'd like to thank you for inviting us over, I hope it wasn't too much of a hindrance."

"Not at all."

"Is there anything I can help you with to lessen your troubles?" Jude asks.

She eyes him with sharp eyes. "You're a charming one, aren't you?"

"I like to think so."

"Uh-huh." She snorts out a laugh. "And yes. You can all help. There's always plenty to get done around here."

She sends Reese and Annabel into the house to get plates, drinks, and the side dishes, while Jude and I are tasked with hosing off the patio table and chairs. Beast's assignment is to help her get the brisket out of the smoker.

"And don't stop with that silver tongue of yours, boy. It's been a while since I've had company to flirt with."

Jude laughs and he even kisses the old lady's hand before gallantly bowing his way off to get the hose.

Granny mutters to Reese when she thinks no one is listening. "You watch out for that one. He could charm the birds out of their nests."

I help Jude with cleaning the all-weather Adirondack chairs. They're made of bulky wood, although they're surprisingly smooth to the touch, each one a different, bright shade of red, green, and blue.

Before too long, Reese and Annabel are bringing out the sides and utensils and Beast and Granny have the meat sliced and laid out on a tray. There are biscuits, beans, greens, and a homemade cherry pie.

We eat in the backyard under the shade of a rustling magnolia tree. And even though we're a motley crew, everyone talks and eats in surprising comfort. After Granny says grace.

She taps Reese on the hand. "Tell me, how did you meet all these fine young people?"

"I'm staying at Jude's house."

Granny nods, her sharp gaze flicking to Jude, then back to her granddaughter. "Just the two of you?"

"No. Beast lives there. And Fitz."

Granny's wily eyes narrow. "So, what you're saying is you're living with three men?"

"Um, er, yes." Two bright flags of color appear on Reese's cheeks.

Granny's mouth is a thin line now, but then she

releases a loud whoop. "Well it's about time you did something good. Or should I say bad." Her laughter is loud and infectious. "You got your eye on any of these fellas?"

"Granny, no." Her blush increases, but the rest of us laugh, the chorus of chuckles accompanied by the clink of silverware on plates.

"Go for the big one. I'd love a big strong man to take care of my little Tootsie Roll."

"Tootsie Roll?" Annabel asks. "Why not Reese's Pieces?"

"Well aren't you a clever one," Granny acknowledges. "It's a funny story about Reese, here."

"No. Please. Don't tell baby stories."

Jude clears his throat. "Well now you're gonna have to tell us. We won't judge. We were babies once too." He grins. "Y'all are still babies in my book."

Granny smiles at Jude. "Tootsie Rolls were her grandpappy's favorite sweet. One day when she was no taller than a weed to a tree, he gave Reese one but told her not to eat it until after we all ate supper. Only minutes later, Reese came out of her room crying because she had already eaten the whole thing. She was so sure she'd be in so much trouble, and Grandpappy was tickled pink at how upset she was over a trifling little thing." Granny laughs. "She's been our little Tootsie Roll ever since."

Reese groans. "Can't we tell embarrassing stories about someone else? Annabel, you got anything good on Fitz?"

"I tried not to hang out with my little brother when

we were growing up. Oh, but he did have the stinkiest feet in the whole world. They were so bad, our momma made him leave his shoes outside."

"At least I didn't pick my nose and eat it until I was twelve," I throw at her.

Annabel sticks her tongue out at me.

"Real mature," I say. "Let's hear more about Reese when she was a kid. Was she always so smart?"

Reese cuts a sharp glance my way.

"Always," says Granny. "That girl came out of the womb with a sense of the world around her. Asked more questions than anyone and was never satisfied until she knew it all. So curious and aware of everything, and yet it was almost too much. Never seen any child so scared to do anything."

Reese and I lock eyes, but she immediately breaks the contact, her gaze dropping to her plate as she fidgets with her fork.

"Scared?" I ask.

"Good sense of self-preservation. Now, some of it was her sister's fault. Scarlett felt responsible for Reese, being that she's six years older. She was so worried Reese would get hurt she made her wear a helmet just to walk around the house. And Reese here loved that helmet. Wore it to bed, like she might fall out and hit herself. Funniest thing you ever saw, a child running around with helmet and knee pads just to go outside and read."

Everyone laughs at Reese's embarrassment, but I fight the urge, not wanting to mortify her further.

Annabel is the next to turn the conversation. “What about you, Jude?”

All eyes focus on the unflappable Jude. I swear he tenses for a second, but maybe I imagine it. He leans back further in his seat. “Not much to tell.”

“Oh, come on, don’t get shy now. Where did you grow up?” Annabel asks.

“Here and there.”

“Very mysterious,” Granny says.

“Or criminal.” Annabel’s eyes narrow. “If you won’t tell us, we’ll make up our own stories.” She taps a finger on her bottom lip. “You’re on the lam.”

“You are mighty interested in my past. Does that mean you’re also interested in being a part of my present and future?”

She ignores him, continuing like he didn’t speak. “You were a gigolo for a rich heiress but she got too needy and you had to bail.”

“I would never run out on my obligations. Especially to a pretty lady.”

Annabel smiles. “Your parents are circus performers.”

“Just as nomadic but not as talented. I would rather hear stories about you, Ms. Annabel.”

She opens her mouth to retort.

“What about you there?” Granny eyes Beast. “Were you always so . . . large? Is that why they call you Beast?”

Beast says nothing, naturally, but his eyes swing over to Jude.

Jude speaks for him. "I would rather hear some stories about Annabel. Fitz?"

"What's a matter there, boy? Cat got your tongue?" Granny ignores Jude, still staring at Beast.

"He doesn't speak, ma'am," Jude explains.

There's a moment of silence except for the leaves rustling overhead. "Perfect. A man of few words. You're welcome here anytime. I don't know about the rest of you yet."

That makes everyone laugh again, and I think even Beast rumbles a little, but it's too low and fast to be sure.

We finish eating, then participate in a group effort to clean up the food and do the dishes. Granny puts together foil-covered plates of leftovers for us to bring back to the house.

"Ma'am, this was the best meal I've had in . . . well, ever," Jude says, rubbing his stomach.

"Good. To show your appreciation, I could use some help in the barn before you go."

"What's in the barn?" Annabel asks.

Granny smiles. "Moonshine."

12

Life is about balance. The good and the bad. The highs and the lows. The pina and the colada.
—Ellen DeGeneres

Fitz

"I'm making pomegranate flavor for the holidays," Granny tells us as we're tromping across the backyard, over the manicured lawn, and back to the giant dark-blue barn behind the house.

Never seen a blue barn.

Annabel lifts her brows. "Pomegranate moonshine?"

"It's festive," Granny insists.

"Is this legal?" Annabel asks.

"I have a license to distill."

"You do?" Now Reese's brows lift.

"Well, I did once. Probably still do. Those things don't go bad." She yanks on the giant barn door.

The yeasty smell of bread mixed with the tart tang of apples hits me as the door swings open. This barn isn't used for animals, obviously, although there are a few stalls. The center of the space is taken over by large metal cylinders, barrels, and plastic tubs. Hoses in different sizes and shapes hang up on one wall alongside various tools. From where we stand near the entrance, it's clear a couple of the stalls have been converted to an office and a storage space.

Brass light fixtures hang from the ceiling, casting an orange hue over the gleaming silver stills. High, inset windows reveal the glow of the setting sun.

"I need some help getting the seeds out of the pomegranates for the mash. Annabel and Jude, y'all can help me with that. Beast, will you use those big arms of yours to grab a couple bags of sugar from the storage stall?"

"What do you need from me?" Reese asks her.

"Why don't you get the still fired up." She nods at me. "Show him where to stick the hose. The mash on the south end should be ready to go."

"You're gonna show me where to stick the hose, huh?" I follow Reese over to the big still in the rear of the barn.

"I'm sure her phrasing wasn't an accident." She pries the lid off the bucket of mash, then gestures to what looks like a small metal fridge nearby. "Will you grab a hydrometer, sample tube, and baster from the sanitizer over there?"

I open it up and glance over the contents. The baster is easy, the sample tube is larger, and I think I find what must be the hydrometer, a glass test tube with measurements stenciled on one side. There's not much else to choose from. I hand them to her. "This it?"

"Yes."

She uses the baster to fill the larger sample cylinder and then puts the hydrometer in the liquid. I crouch down next to her while she spins the tube. "What does this thing do?"

"It measures gravity. The specific gravity of water is one. When we initially set up the mash, it has a higher density because of the sugars. When it ferments, the yeast consumes the sugars, lowering the density and therefore the specific gravity. You'll know it's ready and the fermenting is done when the specific gravity measures less than one."

She points out the reading on the hydrometer and I nod even though I have absolutely no idea what the heck she's talking about.

"It's under, so we should be good to go. Now we transfer it to the still for heating."

Reese directs me to the hoses, and we set one up together, one end in the still and the other in the mash. She shows me how to transfer the liquid over. "What's next?" I ask.

"We heat the still once the mash is in. The heat causes evaporation and condensation—because alcohol has a lower boiling point than water, so boiling filters out the alcohol. When you're done with the hose, put it in the stall over there to be disinfected."

I put the hose away and then watch her light the propane burner underneath the still. "So, this is the whole process?"

"Basically. Inside the still there's a filter. The heat forces the alcohol to separate and the liquid comes out here." She points at a spigot. Underneath is a large barrel. Sure enough, after a few minutes some clear liquid begins trickling out.

"I can't believe you know how to make moonshine."

Although after our conversation last night, I'm not sure anything should surprise me. Reese isn't quite like anyone I know.

She reaches over and grabs a mason jar from a nearby shelf. "You're surprised I can make moonshine? What's more surprising is you don't. This is the South."

"I guess you're right."

She puts a mason jar under the tap to collect some of the liquid before it runs into the bigger bucket underneath. "Do you want to try some?"

"Sure." I glance around. "Where did everyone go?"

"Granny's probably got 'em cleaning out the coop at this point. She's really taken a shine to Beast."

"It is handy to have someone so big around."

"Here." She hands me the jar.

I take a sip and the burn is immediate and powerful and I feel it out through my toes. "Wow."

"Takes some getting used to."

I cough. "You drink this stuff?"

"Sure." She takes a small swig and purses her lips, contemplating the taste. "Not too bad. She's right about the pomegranate, makes it smoother."

I grimace. "Smooth like rubbing alcohol. I don't know how to feel about the fact you can hold moonshine better than I can."

One side of her mouth tips up and my eyes are drawn to the motion. Her lips are wide and pink and still shiny from the moonshine.

She brushes her hair back, one ornery piece that keeps popping into her face. It immediately falls out again and I have to clench my hands to stop myself from reaching out to push it back for her.

"Are you embarrassed?" she asks.

"I don't know. You saw me roll in pig poop. It doesn't get much more embarrassing than that."

She laughs, tipping her head back. "There may have been some excrement on myself as well. I'm not sure who should be more embarrassed."

We share a smile, a sense of familiarity swelling between us like a fast-rising tide.

We're standing so close, I can see a faint freckle below her dark-blue eyes.

It would be so easy to lean forward. See if the moonshine tastes any better coming from her lips.

Her eyes flick down to my mouth and then back up.

The silence stretches on between us, but instead of being our normal, animosity-fueled, quiet friction, another kind of tension reaches out and holds us in its grasp. Heat sinks into me as I imagine what it would be like, the press of her body against mine, the feel of her lips. What would she do if I moved close enough to taste, starting with her mouth, trailing down her neck and to the delicate line of her collarbone? I lean closer, searching her face for clues that she's experiencing any of the same sensations. I can't even control the motion.

Annabel's voice rings out. "Hey, Fitz! Reese? You guys 'bout done? We need help with these seeds." Her words bounce around the space and kill any and all sensation below the belt.

The moment broken, Reese jumps back like she's been shocked, her eyes blinking at me before she turns away.

"Be right there," she calls. And then she hurries away and I have to wait a few seconds, gathering my wits and calming my body before I can follow.

THE RIDE HOME IS JUST AS INTOLERABLE AS THE RIDE there was. I'm still crunched up on Beast's giant lap with my head tilted at nearly a ninety-degree angle, except now we're all full of food, making the space even more cramped.

I can't stop thinking about the strange moment in the barn. Or maybe it was only my strange moment. She didn't seem affected, talking to Annabel and Jude like nothing happened.

I couldn't have imagined it though. Could I?

Annabel drops us off, not even bothering to turn off her car despite Jude asking her to come in for a spell.

It's an odd moment, Jude offering out of normal hospitality, Annabel's shoulders getting tense while she avoids eye contact with everyone. Jude shrugs and exits the vehicle while the rest of us tumble our way out.

Abby left me a note on the front door.

After giving it a glance, Jude hands it to me without a word.

Please call me.

I crumple it up and shove it in my pocket.

It's an unusually quiet night. Beast does the books in the kitchen with Reese. I'm caught up on homework and end up in the living room with Jude, who puts on another romance movie. This one is about two assistants trying to set their bosses up to free up more time for themselves. And of course, they fall in love.

It's not too bad. I would be into it more if Jude didn't keep yelling, "Taye Diggs is the man!" every ten minutes.

My thoughts are too distracting. Reese. Abby coming over. The note she left.

I'm not going to be able to keep her away forever. It might be better to get it over with. I need to tell her to back off and give me space, and I need to do it in a situation I can control.

I stand up and head through the sliding doors and into the backyard. It's weird to be out here when it's empty and quiet.

Phone in hand, Abby's contact information lighting

up the screen, I stare down at her name. Before I can overthink it, I push the call button.

She answers on the third ring. “Fitz. I’m so glad you called. I’ve missed you so much.”

She doesn’t sound drunk at least.

“I’m sorry about the other night,” she says.

“Which one?”

She blows out a harsh breath. “That’s fair. You know I’m sorry about so many things, but I shouldn’t have . . . gone after you after I’d been drinking. It’s just . . . I miss you.”

I swallow. I can’t really say I miss her too. It’s not the truth. “We’re not getting back together, Abby. And I need some space. You gotta stop coming around here.”

“I know, but I miss our friendship. Can’t we be friends again? We were once, you know? We were friends first and always.”

She’s not wrong. An image flashes in my head of Abby in second grade, her blonde hair in pigtails, defending me when another kid accused me of stealing his lunch. “We tried. It didn’t work.”

“I know. And it’s my fault. Tell me what to do. I’ll do anything.” Her voice is earnest, almost desperate.

“I want honesty. Why did you send me that text the other night? The one about going to sleep and not waking up?”

She’s silent for a few long seconds. “That wasn’t a lie. I really feel that way, sometimes.”

I sit in the patio chair. “Why?”

“I don’t know. I can’t explain it, it just is. But then . . .

if people pay attention to me, I feel better. It's like a distraction from bad thoughts, you know?"

"Abby." I clench a hand in my hair, unsure what to do, knowing I need to say something. "You need help."

"I'm not crazy, Fitz."

"I'm not saying you are. I'm saying maybe you should talk to someone about these things, someone who understands."

"I'm talking to you," she huffs.

"I'm not yours anymore."

"I know. I thought I'd never lose you. You never give up, on anyone or anything. You're a great boyfriend and my best friend. I really fucked up. All over the place. And I'm sorry. I hope someday we'll get back to how it used to be."

I'm not sure if she means when we were kids or when we were a couple. I can't see it happening either way.

But I also can't stop the sympathy and concern. She needs help, from a professional, but I'm not sure how to force her to get it. I can't, really, can I?

It's like she's two different people.

There's the Abby she is now, when it's only the two of us, and the one she is the rest of the time. What if this is all more manipulation? The lines are blurred and I can't distinguish her from some stranger. Things have gone too far off the rails.

"I know I've treated you badly," she says. "I don't blame you if you don't wanna talk to me ever again, but I promise I'll do better if you'll stay in my life."

"Talk is cheap. If you can show me you're not just

using me to fill some sick need to control people, maybe someday we can be friends again. But it's going to take a long time. And I still need some space. A few months, at least."

She sniffs a few times, and I harden my heart against her tears. "We've never gone more than a few days without talking." Her voice is small and sad and I have to take a deep breath and stay strong.

"You'll be fine, Abby. You should talk to your parents. Or even someone at the school, maybe a counselor."

She scoffs. "I don't need that kind of help."

I take a deep breath. She's still not listening. "Abby—"

"If it means so much to you, I'll think about it," she cuts me off.

Surprised at her sudden turn, I pause. "Good. I'm glad."

We hang up and I set the phone down next to me on the chair.

I'm raw. Rung out like an old dish towel that should have been trashed three months ago.

Standing, I turn toward the house, and through the window I can see Jude still on the couch, laughing at the movie. Behind him, through the open doorway, Beast and Reese sit at the kitchen table, books spread out in front of them.

Reese pushes back an errant lock of hair and frowns down at something in front of her.

Our moment in the barn comes rushing back and I shut my eyes.

Is it normal to feel attraction to someone so soon? Maybe it's because I've never spent any time with any other woman that I wasn't related to.

I can't be having any kind of feelings for anyone. Right? Isn't there a thing, like a rebound thing that's supposed to be happening?

Maybe that's all it is. Rebound.

Combined with the fact that she is so different from Abby. But not in the way I initially thought.

She's smart. Way smarter than anyone I've ever met. But it's more than that. She cares about her family. She helped Granny even though she pulled a gun on her and won't let her stay in her own home.

I try to imagine Abby's reaction and I know she would have thrown a fit. She's a little spoiled.

Through the window, Reese points out something to Beast in his notebook. Is he actually talking to her? I doubt it. Yet somehow, she's found a way to communicate.

Reese isn't quite like anyone I've ever met.

That must be why, last night, when she told me she'd never been kissed, I wanted to be the first one, the only person in this world to cup her delicate face in my hands. I wanted to rub a thumb over her thick bottom lip and test the color, see if it's as soft as it looks, confirm it with my own mouth.

My teeth grind together.

So many reasons it's a bad idea, and yet the thought won't leave me alone.

13

The two most important days in your life are the day you are born and the day you find out why.

—Mark Twain

Reese

MONDAY, I GET HOME EARLY BECAUSE MY LAST CLASS IS canceled. I run into Jude coming down the front sidewalk on his way out.

"Hey, babies. Perfect timing. I need a ride." He doesn't seem at all surprised to see me.

"A ride?"

"Can you drive me to a friend's house? And then maybe you can help me with a little problem. Come on."

He passes me, walking toward my car where I left it parked at the curb. "I'll explain on the way there."

I have nothing else to do, and to be honest, I'm curious about where he's going and what he could possibly need from me, and so like the inquisitive cat who was inevitably killed, I follow.

Except Jude doesn't really explain much on the way there, only asks me questions about the places I liked to go around town when I was a kid.

"The library is pretty good. The museum is decent, but I sort of memorized all their exhibits by the time I was eight. They need to change it up more."

"Is there anywhere else in town a child with a brain like yours would like to go?"

I consider the question while Jude directs me down a small street on the south side of town, where the properties are small and the homes manufactured.

No doubt there's a reason he's asking me this question, and I imagine it has something to do with our destination.

"Maybe to go see the microscopes on campus."

"Microscopes?"

"Yeah. I wish they'd had them when I was a kid. They started a whole mineralogy lab with funding from the mines. They're using various microscopes to analyze sections of ore to project profitability for mining ventures in certain locations, and to anticipate any problems of a metallurgical nature that may arise during milling and smelting."

"Smelting?"

"Extracting metal from the ore."

"Alrighty then. And just anyone can go in and see these microscopes?"

"Well, no. But one of my professors told us he allows his techs to show them to interested students. I haven't gone yet, though, even though he said we could drop in any time the lab's open."

Ever since I heard they had brought in a probe-corrected scanning transmission electron microscope, I've been dying to go see it, but I have yet to muster up the courage to go to the lab on my own.

"I knew you were the right person to help me with this."

"I'm still not sure what it is I'm helping you with." Although I'm starting to get an inkling.

"Is the lab open today?"

I swallow. "Yes."

"Then you, my dear Tootsie Roll, are going to see those microscopes today." He claps his hands once. "Park here." He motions to a faded and sagging double wide on the right side of the road, and I pull in next to an ancient station wagon. "I'll be right back."

Jude gets out of the car and lopes up a rickety porch.

He doesn't take long. Within moments, he's back with his friend, pulling the seat forward for him to clamber into the back seat.

His friend, who can't be more than ten years old.

I did expect a child, but watching him high-five Jude and crawl into my back seat is still a bit surprising.

"Hello," I say.

"Hi." The kid has dark hair and wide brown eyes. And he's wearing a dark jacket and red tie. The tie has a stain on the bottom and the suit jacket is worn and entirely too large for his thin frame.

Jude gets in the front seat and shuts the door. "Reese, this is Fynn. Fynn, Reese. She's taking us somewhere special today."

"Hello, Fynn."

"Where are we going?" His grin is infectious and wide, his eyes sparkling with interest.

"It's a surprise," Jude says.

"I don't like surprises."

"You'll like this one, I reckon."

I pull out of the driveway, glancing back at Fynn, who's now staring out the window.

"How did you two meet?" I ask.

"Jude's my big brother," Fynn says. "Has been for years."

I lift my brows at Jude.

"Big Brothers Big Sisters. You've heard of it?"

"I have."

Jude continually surprises me, but still, I can't believe he does this. I didn't even know there was a program like this in Blue Falls.

Jude turns in his seat to look back at Fynn. "Reese here is really good at numbers. She can do large sums in her head without a calculator."

"She can?"

"Yep."

I don't understand why Jude is telling him this. What

does it matter? But then Fynn starts to laugh, and his giggle is infectious.

"We should see who's faster." He's bouncing in the back seat now.

"Good idea." Jude turns back around and pulls his phone from his pocket. "Whoever wins the most gets an ice cream cone from the Frostee Freeze. My treat."

And so we spend the entire drive to the university with Jude throwing out numbers and Fynn and I scrambling to answer. It ends up being best out of ten and to my shock and utter delight, Fynn wins.

By the time I've parked near the research building, I'm bouncing in my seat nearly as much as Fynn is.

When we have to cross the street, he takes my hand as if we've been doing this forever. "Do you like science, too?" he asks me.

"I do. I like literature and history as well."

"Eh, not me. I like science and math the best. History is boring."

"Maybe you haven't found topics that are exciting enough."

"Maybe." He doesn't seem convinced. "School can be rather monotonous."

Jude and I meet eyes over his head and I can't help but chuckle.

While we go through the lab, he peppers me and the techs with questions. When the lab tech starts talking about measuring the chemical composition of ore with electron energy loss spectroscopy, Jude's eyes glaze over, but Fynn is just as thrilled and curious as I am about everything and anything.

After, we go for ice cream at the Frostee Freeze and Fynn and I are both chattering like magpies.

The interior is like an old fifties-style diner, all gleaming brass and bright colors with mini jukeboxes at each table that only cost ten cents.

Jude ends up buying us both sundaes and Fynn and I talk. He mostly asks questions about the microscopes. I do my best to answer, and the ones I don't know, I write down and promise to come back with an answer, something that shocks Fynn.

"Momma gets real annoyed when I start asking too many questions. She just tells me to look it up and quit being so chatty. But I can't look it up because we don't have any internet and the library is too far for me to walk."

"Well, I have internet and a library nearby. I'll look it up and get back to you." I'm already thinking about how I can remedy the problem for him. Maybe I can call my parents' manager and set up something through one of their various charities.

Jude doesn't say much, just watches us with a smile and eats his own ice cream cone.

After we drop Fynn off—with promises to bring him some of my old geology books—I have to ask Jude as we're driving back home. "How did you get into doing this whole Big Brother thing?"

"Just kinda fell into it, I guess."

I get the impression I'm not going to get more than

that from him, so I switch tactics. "And how did it happen that my class was canceled right at the time you needed to do your Big Brother thing with Fynn?" Total shot in the dark, but it was extremely unusual that Professor Reyna canceled class. She never misses a lecture. She even taught last month when she had the flu, even though we could barely hear her through the surgical mask.

Jude's gaze hits me, unblinking and sharp as a razor. Okay, there's *definitely* more to Jude Parker than this whole laid-back party guy image he projects. "Just lucky, I guess."

"Really. That's some luck," I say, but don't press him further. "He's a smart kid."

"The best. I knew you two would hit it off."

We drive in silence while I navigate down Main Street. Are there more kids like Fynn? Like me? "Are there others? Like him? Locally, I mean."

"None exactly like him, to be sure, but if you're talking about local kids who have an insatiable curiosity and drive to learn, I would say there are quite a few in need."

My brain is already ticking ahead. What if I could do something big, like open a school for gifted kids in Blue Falls? A thing like that would have changed my whole life. If there are others, kids like me, kids who want to learn everything but no one around them who understands, if I had had that growing up . . .

It doesn't necessarily help me pick my major, but it's a start.

It's still early, not even four. Is my advisor still in her office?

AN HOUR LATER, I LEAVE MY ADVISOR'S OFFICE WITH MORE hope than I've had in a long time.

I'm likely going to have to get at least a master's degree in education, but I've done it. I've picked a major. Er, two. After discussion with the advisor, I settled on a double major in physics and math with a minor in business.

My mind is spinning with possibilities. I won't be able to do it all myself—I might have to use my trust fund to establish the school. And I'll have to hire other like-minded teachers and get students to, you know, enroll. I don't want to have to charge much, if at all, so I'll have to look into getting nonprofit status and potential ongoing funding from the school district, but I've got time. And for the first time, I have a glimmer of hope that I'll be able to do something important with my life. Something where I can continue to learn everything I want about different subjects and also help people who are as different as I am.

But in order to meet this goal, I have to get over my fears. I've already started, but I've got more work to do. No more hiding. No more avoiding people.

Outside the building, I spy Duke heading in the opposite direction.

When we reach each other, he stops to talk to me.

"Hey. You look happy."

"I picked my major. Well, double major."

"What did you settle on?"

"Math and physics."

"Wow." His brows lift in surprise. "That's amazing. You're pretty smart, huh?"

My face heats in sudden embarrassment. "I guess."

"No, don't be shy. You should own your talents. It's great. And you're gonna need those smarts to win the competition tonight because I have my money on you, Einstein." Duke smiles again and his dimple winks at me and he's very cute and attentive but . . . my mind flickers back to yesterday in the barn with Fitz.

Duke doesn't make my heart race like Fitz does. And he can't possibly be attracted to me *like that*. Maybe he just needs a friend. A weird one. Or help with calculus. He looks like one of those guys who's just a big flirt and friendly to everyone. I'm sure it means nothing.

"Where are you headed now? Are you hungry? I'm heading over to the grill for an early dinner. Want to join me?"

I hesitate.

"My treat, to celebrate your new life plan."

The old me would have run away from this whole conversation. Avoiding any possibility of being around people I barely know and—heaven forbid—socializing with them. But that was the old me. I'm turning over a new leaf. No more hiding.

"Sure. Sounds great."

14

Every hero doesn't do this great big hero thing. They do the simple thing over and over, and they stick to it.

—Matthew McConaughey

Fitz

"Did you tell Abby to call Martha? She still hasn't heard from her."

I put the last box of my stuff in the back of my truck and close the tailgate. I can't look at her with a lie on my tongue. "I told her."

I didn't. I forgot. During my last conversation with Abby, I wasn't exactly thinking about our mommas.

"She's okay, right?"

"Of course. She's good. Busy with school and stuff." I turn to face her.

She's watching me with the look that mommas get, like they can see right through you and know everything you've ever done in your entire existence and even some things you've only thought of.

"I think Martha's overly protective," she says after a moment passes. "But you know, that girl has a lot of ups and downs. Hot and cold. Skittish as a beat colt. Never able to handle any stress or hard changes. She's been that way since she was little and she ain't gonna change. Tom wasn't around enough. I know it's helped them financially, but it took a toll on Abby."

Uncomfortable with talking about Abby and keeping our breakup a secret, I change the subject and walk with her back up to the house. "Did Annabel already get her things?"

"She came by yesterday. I know you kids are upset about us moving, but it's time."

"I know. I wish I could help you more."

"Your sister said the same thing." Her smile is fond and a little weepy around the edges. "You kids are the best thing I ever did. You can help me by doing good in school and making sure you call me every Sunday. And you and Annabel can come visit us in Florida. Grandma's house is walking distance to the beach."

I nod and agree and give her a hug. God, she feels so tiny in my arms. What will it be like when she's gone?

By the time I get back to Jude's, it's nearly time for supper.

I find all of my roommates in the kitchen, Jude at the stove. Reese is next to him, chopping something at the counter. It should have been Reese's night to cook, but since we went to Granny's last night, she switched with Jude. It appears she's still helping though.

"Fitz!" Jude bellows as soon as I enter the kitchen. "You are in for a treat tonight. I'm making Jude Parker's famous chili."

"Sounds great."

"There will be plenty since Ms. Reese here already ate dinner and will not be partaking with the rest of us. You can tell her how much she's missing out on."

Reese rolls her eyes. Jude holds out his hand and she passes him a large spoon.

He stirs the pot and eyes me out of the corner of his eyes. "A little birdie told me our little Tootsie Roll here went to dinner with a Mr. Duke Wilson."

Her cheeks flush and she busies herself with cleaning something in the sink.

"Duke?" I ask, instead of what I really want to ask, which is, Who the hell is Duke? And why is she blushing over him?

And why am I suddenly punchy about Reese eating dinner with some guy?

"Well, babies." Jude puts a lid on the pot and wipes his hands on a kitchen towel. "Dinner will be ready in twenty minutes and people are gonna be arriving shortly thereafter. Time for me to get beautiful."

Reese shuts the tap off on the sink and grabs the

towel from Jude. "Do I have to wear anything special tonight?"

"Not unless you want to. Nothing messy will be happening, though, at least not on you. You're gonna love it."

She smirks at him. "You keep saying that, and yet . . ."

"What? You cannot tell me you aren't having the time of your life, Tootsie Roll."

She laughs and flicks at him with the towel. She's different. Relaxed. Happy. Is it because of this Duke character? Is Duke butt-chin man? And why does it bother me so much?

I shove the thoughts away. I have to focus for the next challenge.

An hour later, I've eaten and changed and I'm out in the backyard with the rest of the crowd, awaiting further instruction.

Wading through the crush, I eventually find Reese in what I've determined is her spot, off to the side of the yard near the bushes.

The giant tarp is back. Except this time instead of chutes and ladders, it's a large grid of lettered squares and it's all roped off from the rest of the yard.

"What is this?" Reese asks when I make my way next to her. "Any ideas?"

"Could be anything. Jude is a man of many surprises."

"He really is."

We share a smile and watch the crowd gather together in comfortable silence.

After a few minutes, a strange bleating resonates over the hum of the crowd along with the jangle of . . . bells? We both turn in time to see Beast leading in three baby cows from around the side of the house.

"Is this . . . cow-pie bingo?" I ask, looking at the grid of letters in a new light.

Jude appears from out of nowhere, holding a hand out to Reese, the megaphone clutched in his other hand. "Ms. Reese, you have the key?"

She pulls it from around her neck and hands it over.

And then Jude is on. "Babies! Listen up! You all know this game. We couldn't get any big steers back here without violating about ten county laws and tearing the place up, but the rules are the same. Our competitors will each pick out their squares. Instead of spelling Bingo, we'll be spelling Jude."

The crowd laughs and someone yells out, "You the man, Jude!"

"I won't deny it, babies. Reese, Fitz, you can take turns choosing your squares and since Reese is the reigning champ, she goes first. There are twenty in total so you each get ten."

It doesn't take long to pick our squares out and then Jude nods at Beast. "Y'all ready?"

The crowd screams.

"Release the calves!"

At his words, Beast releases the cows onto the tarp, tying the rope off once they're all in.

All three are a light reddish brown, indistinguishable from each other except their bells are all different colors.

The one with the red bell runs back and forth along the fence line. The other two, one with a blue bell and one green, chase each other near the middle of the roped-off area.

They're kinda cute to watch for the first couple of minutes, but then they settle down, sniffing at the roped-off fence in between playful bouts with each other.

"This is rather anticlimactic," I tell Jude when he approaches us, watching the baby bovines frolic.

Jude is unconcerned. "They're adorable though, aren't they?"

The one in the blue bell is right next to us, and it decides at that moment to drop a steaming pile of crap.

In one of the squares I selected.

"Yes!" I crow. "I have a U."

"That's one letter for Fitz Moreland!" Jude calls out.

Reese purses her lips for a second, then stalks over to the other side of the tarp and starts talking softly to one of the calves and whistling at it.

"Hey, no interfering with the cows, that's cheating!" I call over to her.

"Jude never said we couldn't entice the calves to one of our squares."

"She's right," Jude says. "Cows are stubborn creatures, anyway, she won't get it to—"

"I have a J!" she calls out.

"Well, I'll be."

And so, we spend the next twenty minutes cajoling the cows to various squares in the hopes they'll poop and get us the letters we need. We're at a tie, each only needing one final letter.

"If you come over here, cow, I'll never eat veal again," I say to the cow with the red bell.

"Moo," he responds.

"Stop bribing the calves."

"You started it."

Our bickering gets the cow all twitchy and then he poops. And it's right in the square I need.

"I have a D!" I lift both hands in the air.

"We have a winner for the fourth round of Bedlam!" Jude announces into the megaphone.

People cheer and crowd toward me. Jude hands off the key, and I catch a glimpse of Reese's back as she disappears toward the house.

Where is she going?

A few guys clap me on the back with offers of beer, but I wave them off and follow the path Reese made. I don't want her to leave. I want to talk to her more, see what she thinks now that we're tied in the competition. And I just . . . want to be around her.

I catch up with her near the back door. "Hey, I know I interfered with your time in the room when you won, and I wanted to let you know I'm willing to share."

Her cheeks flush before I realize how that sounds. "I mean, not like share like that, but you know the way we did . . . before." I grimace and rub the back of my head. "This isn't coming out right."

She laughs. "I get what you're saying, and while I

appreciate the offer, I think I'll take the floor if it's okay with you."

"The floor?"

"Yeah. I can scrounge up some extra blankets and pillows, make it real cozy. You'll have to make sure you don't step on my head."

"Right." I pull the key over my head and hand it to her.

She blinks, surprised.

"So you can get in now, if you want."

Her mouth opens but before she can answer, revelers step between us, shouting and laughing and pushing at each other.

When they finally move past us and into the house, she's gone.

BY THE TIME I MAKE IT TO BED, REESE IS ALREADY IN there, on the floor like she said.

The Christmas lights are on, and her eyes are open.

"Hey."

"Hey."

I step over her carefully, getting on the bed before tugging my shirt over my head.

Making a lady sleep on the floor while I have the bed gives me a sick stomach, and I tell her as much.

"You won fair and square. If I had won, I wouldn't be feeling any guilt. I might be reveling in my win, actually."

I laugh. "Yeah, you're a big gloater. It still seems wrong, I mean you're a . . ."

"Girl? That's sexist."

I chuckle. "I know, I know. Still, this whole situation is basically my fault."

"It wasn't just you. Abby had a lot to do with it." Her voice is hesitant.

I lie back on the bed, sinking into a heavy pause while anxiety and awkwardness at the mention of Abby float in the air above us. She continues in a rush, "And to be honest, if I had stuck up for myself or said something to someone when she first started causing problems, I might not be here right now. So really, there isn't any one person to blame."

My body tenses as she speaks and I have to force myself to relax. Part of me has known for a while now that Abby isn't the kindest person, but having it confirmed is like an extra sucker punch just when you think the fight is over. "It's okay, you can talk about Abby. I'm not holding on to any false illusions about who she was. Is. Who she is. I guess I'm embarrassed I had my head stuck in the mud as long as I did."

"It was nothing truly awful. I mean, she said awful things, but it was mostly passive-aggressive stuff. She didn't, like, put black dye in my toothpaste or fire ants in my pillowcase."

That makes me chuckle. "Well thank God for that."

"I'm just saying, you have nothing to feel bad for. You aren't her."

"Yeah, but I was with her for years. I defended her. Let her suck me into her bullshit."

She shuffles on the floor and then her head appears at eye level. "You aren't responsible for someone else's bad behavior. No matter your relation to them."

Something tight in my gut unclenches. It's a freeing thought, not being responsible for Abby anymore. "I guess you're right."

"Besides, it's nothing I'm not used to." She lies back down, her head disappearing. "It's just that I never had to *live* with a bully before. It was harder to ignore, but I managed."

And there goes my gut, clenching again. "What do you mean? When were you bullied?"

"It was, you know, silly kid stuff in high school."

"Wait. Didn't you go to Blue Falls?"

"Yeah."

I can't believe that Reese has lived this life in Blue Falls, this existence that's so separate from my reality, and I never knew. Never saw her. Never stepped in for her. "Who picked on you?"

She sighs. "It wasn't a big deal. Once I learned how to be invisible, they stopped."

Now I'm not sure what's worse, that she's so pragmatic about having to hide who she is, or the fact that I can't go back in time and do something about it. "Who is they?"

"Does it matter?"

"Yes, because if they're still around, I can find them and scissor kick them in the face."

She laughs.

"What's funny?"

"It's mighty kind of you, Fitz, but really it's nothing to be concerned about. There were some snide comments and laughter at my expense, but it didn't last long. I'm sure it's because I started school late and had no idea how to act around people."

At Granny's, just the other night, everyone laughed at Reese's discomfort. More guilt wiggles its way inside me. "Why is that?"

"I spent most of my life at home studying and having private tutors, but after I turned fifteen my parents made me go to school. They said I needed to be socialized. They weren't wrong. But I leaned quickly it was best to stay under the radar. Especially since college started and I've had to live amongst all you normies." Her voice is teasing, and I use that glimmer of humor to smother the tension simmering inside me, the sadness at how Reese has been treated and the helplessness at not being able to change any of it. At least not in the past. But in the here and now? And the future?

"Normies, huh?" I ask. "Does that include me?"

"Yep. You're a total normie. Popular, athletic, handsome."

"You think I'm handsome?"

Silence. Maybe I shouldn't have gone there but I can't stop the smirk on my face spreading into a full-blown smile. "I bet you're so red right now."

"At least I didn't say you're *not unattractive*." She

deepens her voice to imitate my speech, making me laugh.

The more she talks, the more she reveals these little pieces of herself, the more I want to know. So I have to ask, "Why did they wait so long to put you in school? You've lived in Blue Falls your whole life, right?"

"Yeah. I don't know. I think initially, they thought tutors would be best for their lifestyle. Sometimes we would travel with them and a nanny, of course, but most of the time Scarlett watched over me. I never really had kids my own age to play with. I wasn't a normal kid right off the bat though. I never really played like kids do in the mud or whatever. I mostly wanted to read."

I laugh. "Not all of us were like Begonia as kids. We did more than just roll around in the mud."

"You know what I mean, I've watched those family movies. Kids are always playing sports, riding bikes, going to the park. I didn't like the park, it was a death trap."

I crack up. "A death trap?"

"Seriously, plunging down a metal slide onto cement? Rotating hunks of metal with chipping paint? A jungle gym that has likely been the cause of numerous broken bones and ER visits?"

"Granny wasn't kidding about the helmet, was she?"

Her voice is full of laughter. "That wasn't even the half of it. I blame Scarlett. One time I fell and skinned my knee under her watch and Granny got so spittin' mad I thought Scarlett would cry for a full year. She never let me do anything even remotely dangerous after that. She would tell me stories about kids falling and breaking their heads open just by walking around outside."

"That's funny. My dad loved to freak us out when we were kids. You know those yellow signs with pictures of cows on the side of the road? When there's open-range steer?"

"Yeah."

"He would tell Annabel and I those were warnings for carnivorous cows."

She laughs. "And you believed him?"

"I was six."

Once her chuckles die down, she asks, "Is your dad okay?"

Thoughts of my parents send a pang down my spine. But I brush it off. "Yeah. He's fine. He's . . . he got hurt at work and has been out on workers' comp. Momma tries to downplay it, but I think it's worse than they're letting on. He sleeps all the time. I barely see him anymore. And now they have to sell their house."

"I'm sorry," she murmurs.

"It's fine. They'll be okay. They're going to live in Florida with my grandma. They'll be able to stay with her, help out, and scrape by on their retirement. I still worry about them though. I know they're struggling with medical bills, even after insurance, and I really want to help them, but right now . . . I feel helpless. It's why I'm majoring in engineering."

"How does majoring in engineering help your parents?"

"It's the field with the highest-paying jobs you can get with a four-year degree."

"Do you like the classes?"

"They're okay."

"If money didn't matter, what would you do?"

The question stops me. It's not something I've ever considered. It's not really about me, it's about taking care of the people I care about the most. "I . . . I don't know. I've never let myself think that way. I pick a course and stick to it."

"So later, if they don't need your help, would you do something else?"

"Sure. Life's not always a straight line from A to B." I've never talked to Abby about these things. I've never talked to anyone. For some reason, Reese is easier to talk to.

"You wouldn't be a professional runner?"

I crack out a laugh. "Not exactly an option. I'm not talented enough. The only reason I've gotten as far as I have with running is because of sheer determination. I do distance running. I've never been a sprinter. I'm not in it for the quick win. I like the skill that comes from endurance. The challenge."

"What made you want to run in the first place?"

I almost don't tell her. I hate to keep bringing her up. But something tells me she would prefer the truth rather than avoiding the tough topics. "Abby."

"Really?"

I was right, her voice rises. But there's no hostility in

it, even though I've brought up the main reason we're in the predicament we're in.

"She wanted to do it but not alone, so I went with her. But then after the first season I sort of fell in love with it."

"That's nice," she says on a yawn.

"Thanks for not being weird."

She laughs. "But Fitz, I am weird."

"I mean, thanks for not being weird when I bring up Abby. I know she's not the easiest person. To be around or to discuss."

"Is it still hard for you to talk about her?"

"Oddly . . . no. I thought it would be worse, actually, but it's not. I mean, she was a big part of my life." She still is, in the sense that I'm still lying to my parents for her and we're still . . . friends? Or could be again, someday. I'm still worried about her and her erratic behavior. "But I think she might have been right. She said something about us being friends first and not really meant to be as a couple. Maybe I always knew, and I wasn't really hanging on to her, but to the idea of her."

"The idea of an epic love story."

"Yes. Exactly. But we've talked enough about me. Have you narrowed your choices down for your major?" I ask.

"Actually, yes, I have."

I can hear the smile in her voice and it prompts me to lean over the side of the bed to look at her. "That's great, Reese."

She's lying on her side, her head turned to grin up at me. "Jude took me to meet a friend of his today. A kid, actually. A really smart kid. I decided I want to open a school someday. For gifted and talented children in Blue Falls."

"That would be amazing."

"I think so."

We smile at each other for a few seconds before I lie back down and stare up at the Christmas lights.

The conversation stalls, but it's not an uncomfortable stretch of silence. It's kind of nice, actually, being able to talk to someone about anything and everything without a fight or any kind of fear of recrimination.

She really is nothing like Abby.

"I'm glad we're friends," I say.

She doesn't respond. But I think I hear a soft breath.

I lean over the side of the bed again.

Reese is curled up on her side, facing in my direction. Her dark lashes cast a shadow over her pale cheek, her hair a riot of sleek, dark waves spread above her.

She's really quite beautiful. In all the ways that matter.

15

Life itself is worth living for. If you're not living the life that you want, you fight for that life.

—Jensen Ackles

Reese

For the first time in, well, ever, I can't wait for class to be over, and I head immediately to Jude's once my last class concludes.

I tell myself it's because it's not a competition day and I'm looking forward to a quiet night for once, but it's not entirely the truth.

The truth is, I can't wait to see Fitz.

We're actually—dare I say it?—friends.

"So, what's up with you and Fitz?"

Speaking of friends, Annabel has become a common fixture at Jude's as well.

We're sitting on the back deck, enjoying the late-afternoon breeze while lounging on a couple of ragtag patio chairs.

It's Fitz's turn to cook and he's grilling burgers and hot dogs. Luckily for me, he's inside getting the cheese for the burgers and a drink for me, so he misses Annabel's probing question.

I glance at the open sliding door before turning back to Annabel. "Nothing is up with us."

"Y'all hated each other and yet now everyone's all cozy, sleeping in the same room, acting like the best of friends."

"Hardly the best of friends."

"Boloney. He asked if you needed anything before going inside and completely ignored his own sister. I'm family. And I'm thirsty."

"You've also sided with me during this whole thing and not Fitz."

She waves a hand. "Eh. We're not talking about Fitz and *me*, we're talking about Fitz and *you*."

Beast ducks through the patio door and hands Annabel a glass of ice water before moving off to a chair on the side of the deck.

"How do you know these things?" Annabel yells at him.

Jude comes out behind him, Mr. Bojangles curled up in one arm. "He's not deaf, Bel."

"Stop calling me Bel."

"Would you rather I call you Anna?"

"Ugh no, I would prefer you call me by my actual name."

"At least he doesn't call you babies." Fitz pops out behind Jude, serving plate in one hand and a glass of water in the other. He hands me the glass before heading over to the grill, setting the platter to the side and popping the lid open. "Why *don't* you call her babies? You call everyone else that."

Jude shrugs. "When's dinner ready?"

Fitz and I share a raised-brow glance.

He totally avoided the question.

"Few minutes," Fitz says.

"I'm famished."

Dinner is eaten outside, balancing paper plates on our laps while Jude and Annabel bicker and Fitz and I share smiles and Beast . . . well, he eats and listens, I suppose.

The breeze tickles my nose and I shut my eyes to enjoy the sun. When I open them again, Fitz and I lock eyes and share a smile and something flutters in my stomach.

"You're ridiculous," Annabel says to Jude and then she flicks a piece of her salad at him and without missing a beat, he catches it in his mouth.

I laugh.

I'm going to miss this.

No matter which way you cut it, one of us is going to be gone next week.

"WE HAVE SOMETHING SPECIAL TONIGHT, BABIES. LASER tag!"

The backyard has been transformed.

Planks of wood have been cobbled together into makeshift walls, and various inflatables and giant wine barrels are strewn about, along with old tires and the kiddie pool, which is now full of water.

We're standing beside Jude on the porch while he yells at the "babies" through his megaphone. Since the yard is being used, everyone's assembled on the deck and in the living room, listening through the open sliding glass door. The crowd grows each time we have one of these. The bets have already been placed, and now Jude is going over the details for the challenge.

"Each of our players will get a gun and a vest. The vests are set up to flash and emit a loud, unique sound when you get shot by your opponent. Three shots and you are out. I have a scorecard here that's wirelessly connected to your vests." He holds up a square black object. It resembles a toy-car remote, except bigger. "So we'll be able to keep track of each hit. Beast?"

Beast slides onto the porch, coming out of the darkness like a killer submarine emerging from the deep.

"Ladies first," Jude says.

Beast holds the vest up so I can stick my arms in the holes and then he fastens me in.

"Don't get too crazy out there, babies. I don't want my biggest sources of income to get injured."

The crowd laughs.

"Your concern is touching," Fitz says drily.

Beast helps him into his vest and then hands each of us our guns.

"Fitz, Reese. Please step into the yard."

We jump off the porch onto the grass.

"A demonstration, if you will! Fitz, go ahead and shoot Reese in the chest."

He hesitates.

"It's a laser gun, not a real gun. You aren't gonna hurt her. Just do it."

He pulls the trigger. My vest lights up orange and makes an obnoxious yodeling sound, much to the delight of the audience.

"Now you," Jude tells me.

I don't hesitate, shooting Fitz right in the heart. His vest lights up bright yellow and emits a jarringly loud rooster crowing, eliciting more laughter and claps from the assembled group.

Jude holds up his scoring machine to show the crowd what it looks like on his tablet. "I will reset this bad boy and give a big thanks to the engineering department for designing these wonderful toys. Now then, babies, let the games begin!"

As soon as he finishes his sentence, the entire backyard plunges into darkness.

I can't see anything. It's pitch-black. People are still on the porch, talking and laughing, so I move away, onto the course. I trip over something and then all of a sudden, colorful lights are flashing all around, reds and blues and yellows and greens—like I've been dropped into a disco ball.

At first, I think I've been hit. My stomach drops and I hide behind a barrel. But there's no yodeling, so I suppose I've still got three shots in me. The lights cease and the yard pitches into blackness again.

Jude didn't mention the addition of a sporadic light show. Should make things more interesting. Now that I somewhat have my bearings, I'll have to use the light show to find Fitz and take him down.

But before I can do more than catch my breath, my vest lights up and a loud yodel fills the night air. People on the porch cheer and laugh.

I've been hit.

"Ouch, Reese," Jude's megaphone sounds from the porch. "That's one hit for Fitz. Zero for Reese."

The disco lights flash again and I glance around the yard, but I can't see Fitz anywhere.

I didn't hear him move.

He probably knows exactly where I am too, since he just shot me and I haven't budged so I need to be getting a move on.

I circle one of the barrels, staying low and listening. The lights turn off and I'm about to make a run for a wall nearby when my vest lights up and once again the yodeling startles me into a laugh.

"Two hits now for Fitz Moreland! Only one more hit and you're out, Tootsie Roll," Jude's voice echoes over the backyard.

Darn it all to Dante.

The lights flash again and I use the opportunity to make a run for better cover, glancing around as I do so, on the lookout for any movement. Trying to get myself out of the lights brings me to my favorite place to hide.

I get behind one of the bushes and settle with my back to the fence, considering strategy. The lights click off again, but not before I catch Fitz's head over one of the partitions.

I take aim and shoot, gratified when the distinct sound of a rooster crowing sounds.

"One hit for Reese! Score is now two to one in favor of Mr. Moreland," Jude's megaphone echoes over the yard.

The crowd yells, some cheering, some booing and yelling, "Come on, Reese!"

The lights click on again but I don't see any movement from this vantage point.

After a few seconds, the yard is once again plunged into darkness.

And that's when I hear it—footsteps, right next to my hiding spot.

Before I can make a run for it, my gun is knocked loose and he's right in front of me.

My weapon is on the ground somewhere, the fence to my back and Fitz's gun pointed straight at my vest.

Nowhere to hide.

Fitz's leans into me, despite the gun between us. "You lose." His voice is low and gravelly.

Dangerous. If danger includes the sounds of yodeling and roosters.

"Not yet," I say.

"You can't win. You don't even have a gun anymore."

"You can only fail if you stop trying." I repeat his words back at him from Begonia Day.

He chuckles. "Good."

The lights go crazy again, but I barely notice. We're in a darkened part of the yard so the flashing doesn't quite reach us. The sounds of people out in the yard laughing and partying fade away. The heat of his gaze trails a line down my face, to my lips.

One of his hands, the one not holding the gun, cups the side of my face, his thumb rubbing over my cheek and then lower, tracing my bottom lip.

"Reese." His voice is a low murmur in the dark and I'm leaning toward him like he's reeling me in with a tractor beam.

My hand lifts to cover his, holding it there against my face as I lift up on my toes.

Yodel-ay-hee-whoooo!

I jerk back as my vest lights up and the yodeling shrieks between us.

Jude yells, "We have a winner!"

Fitz is already moving away from me. The porch lights flood on, filling the backyard with bright light.

My eyes meet Fitz and his brows lift and he's staring at the gun in his hand like it's suddenly morphed into a Whataburger. "I didn't mean to . . ."

I don't know if he finishes the sentence because people have infiltrated the space and are cheering and stepping in between us.

Jude's there, handing the key to Fitz, lifting his arm in the air and declaring him the winner of the fifth challenge.

There's the usual applause and groans from the winners and losers and I realize we only have two more to go. It's three to two and Fitz is up by one. I have to win the next two or I'm sunk.

My stomach churns in agitation. Memories flash in my head, pulsing like the laser tag lights. Fitz's warm hand on my face, his thumb on my lips. Restlessness makes me pull away from the crowd. A strange sense of anticipation fills me, like a sneeze that won't materialize. I'm teetering on the brink of something.

If he hadn't accidently shot me, would we have kissed? Would we have kissed in the barn the other night if we hadn't been interrupted?

Clearly, there's an attraction there, but I don't know what to do with it. From what I've observed of others, most people don't think twice about acting on lustful moods with random hookups and then moving on the next day, but I'm not sure it's something I can do. Or something I want to do.

I catch sight of Annabel in the crowd and head toward her.

On my way through the throng, I pass Abby. She doesn't see me, focused on a point to the side. I follow her gaze. Of course, she's staring at Fitz. He doesn't see her, talking to Jude and a few other people.

She's not drunk this time, but she does look exhausted—not wearing her normal layer of makeup.

Her hair is pulled back instead of styled. Her jeans are cute, but her hoodie sweater dwarfs her narrow frame.

I look away in time to see Annabel disappear through the back-patio door and I follow.

Once I make it inside, I can't find her in the living room. She's not in the kitchen either.

But Duke is.

"Einstein!" He's there, in my space, cup in hand. "Come have a drink. I bet you need one."

"Maybe. I'll be back in a sec."

Where the heck did Annabel go? I check down the hall in the bathroom but she's not in the line and there's no way she would be in there already with the number of people waiting.

The door to our room is still locked, so, following a hunch, I head down the back of the house where Jude's and Beast's rooms are. I'm sure they are locked up like ours, but Annabel and Jude have something going on, despite what she says. Maybe he gave her a key?

As soon as I turn down the darkened, empty hallway, I know Jude never gave Annabel a key.

Because she's crouched in front of his door and trying to break in.

"Annabel," I scold.

She jumps and turns, a hand to her chest. "Holy baby Jesus, Reese! You scared me!"

"Good. What in cotton-pickin' Judas are you doing?"

"Nothing." She stands straighter, raising her chin at me.

"Why are you trying to break into Jude's room?"

"I was looking for Mr. Bojangles."

I roll my eyes. "You were not."

"What are you doing here?"

"Don't try and turn this around on me, I was following you."

"Why were you following me?" She crosses her arms over her chest.

"Because I wanted to talk to you about . . ." I smack her on the arm. "Quit trying to change the subject! You are too good at this verbal swordplay."

"I know." She smirks. "And while you excel at almost everything, subterfuge is clearly not your strong point. So, what did you want to talk about?" She steps closer, all business. "How you and my brother almost made out in front of a crowd of onlookers?"

Warmth flashes up my neck, like a cup of fire thrown in my face. "Did everyone see?"

"Only people with thermal-sensor capabilities on their phones."

"How . . . what . . . why?"

"Don't worry, I think there were only a few people who have that app. But I do think Abby was watching over someone's shoulder."

I swallow. "Are you telling me I nearly had my first kiss in front of a hundred people in a backyard while playing laser tag . . . for a bedroom to sleep in . . . and is this how this is supposed to work?" My voice escalates as I speak.

"Calm down, Tootsie Roll. Not many people saw. And first kiss? Girl, you need to get some."

"I'm just confused. I don't know what to do. I'm not sure I can do casual."

"Well, Fitz doesn't do casual either. But what does it matter? Do you like him?"

"I don't hate him. I don't know how I feel. He just broke up with his childhood sweetheart and we're competing against each other."

"Listen. Reese. I know you don't have a lot of life experience, but Fitz is a good guy. You should go with it, whatever you're feeling. Or not feeling. Who cares? Do what makes you happy. You only live once. And for God's sake, kiss someone already. Anyone'll do."

"You really think so? Even though you don't believe in love?"

"Who said anything about love? You could use a distraction. Just because you're competing over a room doesn't mean you can't like each other. It's your life. There are no rules."

Is that all I would be though? A distraction? How does she know he doesn't do casual? Because he hasn't before? Maybe since he's done the long-term thing, he wants something different. I'm completely out of my depth.

"Right. No rules. Okay. Thanks, Annabel."

I've lived my whole life playing it safe, staying away from people, sticking to my little, comfortable bubble and following the path of least resistance. But now that I've strayed onto the road less traveled, I've learned that most people aren't as bad as I once thought. As a matter of fact, I would consider all my roommates to be friends.

Annabel too. For the first time in my life I have friends that I'm not related to.

"You're welcome."

What she's saying makes sense, but I still have so many questions. "So how do I let him know that I'm interested in . . . no rules?"

She blinks at me. "Are you asking me how to seduce someone? I mean, I am all about sexual freedom, but this is my brother we're talking about."

"It's just that, in the animal kingdom, it's typically the male that preens and displays colorful feathers to attract the female. Unless we're talking about seahorses, in which case the female does a dance. What do I do?"

"I don't know." Her hands flail in frustration. "Tell him about those seahorse mating habits."

I frown. "Do you really think that will work?"

She rolls her eyes. "It will if you're naked. Reese, he's a dude. They aren't complex."

"Oh."

"Do you have any bobby pins?"

"What? No. I will not aid and abet you in whatever secret stuff you're doing. Jude is a good guy too, you know."

"Maybe he is, but he's hiding something."

"What could he be hiding?"

"That's what I'm going to find out."

Now that I consider Jude a friend, I'm not sure I can countenance whatever Annabel's got cooking. "I don't want him to get hurt."

"I'm not going to hurt anyone. I'm just looking for the truth."

"I know but . . . sometimes the truth hurts."

I LEAVE ANNABEL TO HER BAD DECISIONS AND HEAD BACK out to the party to make my own.

I'm prepared to go out and find Fitz and talk to him about . . . everything, I guess, but before I make it through the back slider, I spot Fitz and Abby talking on the edge of the yard. Clearly consumed in whatever they're discussing.

Abby's face is stark and earnest and Fitz is completely focused on her.

Doubt fills me. They have a history that I shouldn't get involved in.

I know he said he's not going back to her, but . . . what if he changes his mind?

"There you are. I got you a drink." Duke is suddenly right next to me, too close in the crowded space, handing me a bottle of beer.

I drag my eyes away from the scene outside the window. "Thanks." I pop open the lid using the edge of the bookshelf and take a long drink before wiping my mouth with the back of my hand.

"You okay?" He nudges me with his shoulder.

"I'm fine."

"Is the beer okay?"

"I guess. I don't drink very much. Only when I have to."

His eyes crinkle at me. "And when do you *have* to?"

"To test the moonshine."

A surprised chuckle escapes him. "You're full of surprises, aren't you? Tell me, Einstein, what do you know about poker? Can you play?"

Granny taught me when I was six and I've been beating her nine out of ten times ever since. It wasn't hard once I figured out how to calculate the odds and count cards in my head. Statistically, it isn't a guaranteed win, but it does increase your chances.

"I can."

"Do you want to play with us, or are you gonna break my heart again?"

"When did I break your heart before?"

"Well, you know I've been betting on you every time and you've lost the past two Bedlams."

"Sorry about that."

"Hey, no biggie. You can make it up by playing a couple games with me." His smile is slow and assured.

I shoot a glance back into the yard.

The crowd moves and shifts and there's Abby again. Still with Fitz. Leaning into him. His hand is on her arm as they head around the side of the house.

I smile at Duke. "I can play."

16

I have decided to stick with love. Hate is too great a burden to bear.
—Martin Luther King Jr.

Fitz

Immediately after the laser tag, Reese disappears into the crowd.

I have no idea what's going on with us. Well, actually, I know exactly what's going on and I want to pick up where we left off before I accidently shot her.

But instead of seeing her in the throng of partiers, I see a different female who's the opposite of what I want.

Abby.

She's with Kevin.

His face is a thundercloud and hers is wan and tired but it's an improvement over hammered and stumbling.

She says something to him that makes the thundercloud darken into a hurricane, and he storms off.

But still . . . she doesn't quite look like herself. After our talk the other night, I thought she was doing better. Even though I don't want to ask, I have to.

"Abby, what are you doing here?"

"I know you don't want to see me. Kevin picked me up earlier and I swear I didn't know he would bring me here."

I'm not sure I believe her, but now that she's in front of me and looking so unlike her normal self, I have to ask. "You all right?"

"Fine. Just a little tired. I've been up late. Catching up on schoolwork so I can come clean to the parents." She smiles weakly.

I don't know if I've ever seen her this . . . casual. She'd put on full makeup to go pick up a gallon of milk at the H-E-B.

"Don't work yourself too hard," I say. But then I also remember Momma's words the other night. "I'm sure you'll be able to catch up in no time."

She smiles weakly. "Then once I tell my parents everything, you can move back home and you won't have to do this anymore."

"That would be nice, but it's not happening either way. They're selling the house."

Her eyes widen. "What?"

"They want to downsize now that Annabel and I are out and grown."

She knows some of it, like that Dad has been out of work on injury, but she doesn't know the money struggles. It's not something I've ever really shared with her. It's the kind of thing she would judge. She always had whatever she wanted growing up and wouldn't understand what it's like being truly in dire straits.

Although . . . Reese's parents are loaded too, but it's different with her.

She bites her lip. "I'm sorry, Fitz. I didn't know. I've been avoiding my parents' calls so I hadn't heard." She takes my hand and gives it a gentle squeeze.

But it doesn't feel right.

It's something we've done since we were practically in diapers, and yet . . . it doesn't sit well.

I pull my hand from her grasp. "It is what it is. Hopefully I'll be able to stay here at least for the semester."

She swallows. "This is all my fault."

I don't know what to say. I can't deny it.

Some shirtless dude on the laser tag field yells, "I am a golden god!" and belly flops into the shallow kiddie pool. Abby uses the distraction to move closer, taking my arm and leaning into me like she used to when she had the right.

"Abby." I shrug her off and take a step back, nearly running into someone moving behind me. "Don't do that."

Her face crumples. "I still want us to be friends, you know?"

My words were a hit and I know it, but I can't lead her on either.

I wait for her to compose herself, shoving my hands in my pockets and glancing around at the other revelers. I spot Reese inside, by the sliding door, talking to that guy—Sir Butt-Chin or whatever. As I'm watching, he nudges her with his shoulder, leaning into her space.

"Does it make you mad?" Abby asks, and my attention snaps back to her.

"What?"

"You're frowning. You don't want to be friends?"

"I . . . we already talked about this, Abby. I need space."

"It's because of her, isn't it?" Her tone twists, along with her lip.

"What?"

"When I saw you looking at . . . *her*." She sniffs and wipes her nose with the sleeve of her sweater. "Looking at her like . . . like you *like* her. But you can't, can you? Do you? She's so weird. She's the biggest dork." Her eyes meet mine, still wet with tears, but accusatory now.

Something simmers and wells up inside. Anger. Not for me, but for Reese.

Reese didn't even want to admit how terribly Abby had been treating her, trying to protect me from the truth. Even after the truth came out, Reese could have said any number of things, but she kept it neutral. And here Abby is, the culprit playing the victim, and she's trash-talking *Reese*?

"She's not a dork. She's actually pretty cool. You lived

with her for a year. Did you ever even try and talk to her?"

"Well. No." My words fluster her. She blinks rapidly and then searches my eyes. "She's not normal, Fitz."

My jaw clenches as it hits me. Really hits me, exactly what Reese said about us *normies*. And what she must have gone through for years. People not understanding her, not seeing her. And why? Because she refused to be exactly like the rest of us? Because she talks smart and doesn't try to fit in?

"Just because she's not into partying and failing school while lying and cheating on her boyfriend doesn't mean she isn't normal."

She gasps. "You do like her, don't you?" She's shaking her head. "This ain't right, Fitz. She's not the one. It's supposed to be me. You were always supposed to be my forever guy. Remember? Ever since third grade." Her voice is rising.

I can't have this. People are watching. "We can't talk about this now." I keep my voice low, moving closer so she can hear me, taking her arm and trying to lead her around the side of the house, where it's darker and quieter. And there's an exit through the garage. "Maybe you should go. Go with Kevin. You came here with him."

She takes my hand on her as an invitation, moving closer, leaning into me again.

"Kevin doesn't mean anything to me. You're the only one that matters, the only one that makes me feel . . . real."

"What are you talking about? You're not making any sense."

Although . . . in a weird way, she kinda is. Abby has always been a flirt, always thrived when the focus was on her, especially focus of the male variety.

She stops our progression and we haven't even made it around the corner when Kevin appears out of the crowd, stalking toward us. I'm more grateful than I thought I would be to see his stupid face.

"We should get out of here." He puts an arm around Abby's shoulders.

I'm about to agree with him, but then Abby shrugs off Kevin's arm, stepping away. "You don't tell me what to do," she snaps.

"I'm leaving and I'm your ride, so you can come with me now or walk your ass home."

Abby sputters and cries and screeches, and yet I don't hear her response. I watch them fight and it's like a movie where the sound has been turned down and everything goes slow-motion because in a moment of perfect clarity, I realize this is what I've escaped. This was my life, before.

I didn't fight with Abby, and this is what she wanted. The high drama, the attention all focused on her, and when I wouldn't give it to her, she went elsewhere for it.

They don't say goodbye or pay me any attention, continuing to argue even as they're walking away, around the side of the house and out of view.

I wouldn't bring the drama for her and it's what she wants. But it's not what I want.

That's not an epic love story, that's an epic disaster.

Heading back into the yard, I look for Reese. She isn't standing in the open doorway anymore.

I would have kissed her. In front of everyone. I want her. Badly. Worse than I ever wanted Abby. There's no artifice, no drama or lies, just her. She's so completely herself, awkwardness and ridiculousness and all.

And with that thought, I head inside to find her, excitement thrumming through my veins like a drum beat.

Until I find her in the kitchen. At the small table, surrounded by three guys, all in various stages of undress.

"What's going on in here?" I step up to the table, getting in between Reese and the butt-chin guy, who also happens to be the least dressed one. He's in only boxers.

"Strip poker. I'll take two." She tells the dealer and switches out her cards. "Do you know Duke?" And yes, she motions to Sir Butt-Chin.

"No. Hey." I nod at him and his buddies at the table. One is in a shirt and boxers, and one has no shirt but is still in his pants.

"Want in on the next round?" Duke asks me. "I'll be naked in ten seconds with this card shark here." He leans around me to pat Reese on the arm and I have the inexplicable urge to break it.

Unaware of the feelings swirling inside me, Reese speaks. "The original term is actually card *sharp*, which referred to someone who cheats at cards. The phrase card *shark*, however, evolved soon after and isn't necessarily pejorative. It can refer to anyone who has any kind of legitimate skill with cards, even for entertainment purposes."

Duke laughs, leaning even closer to Reese even though I'm definitely in the way. "Is there anything you don't know?"

Reese shrugs. "You don't know what you don't know."

Duke is looking at her like he wants to eat her up, and Reese doesn't seem to mind.

He gets even closer and now his bicep pushes against my side and I can't help but push back a little, even though it's the height of immaturity. I don't care.

He pushes even harder and I step into Reese, forcing his arm to the side with a jerk. A Solo cup spills and the liquid runs in Reese's direction all over her white T-shirt.

"Oh shoot." She shoves her chair back, but the damage is done.

The other players all scramble for napkins to sop up the beer and save the cards. I grab the roll of paper towels and hand it over. When I try to hand some to Reese, she waves me off, holding the shirt up a bit and exposing the pale line of flesh above her jeans.

"It's fine, I'll run and change."

"I have the key."

"Right."

I hand off the towels and follow Reese through the crowd and down the hall to the room.

Pulling the key off my neck, I unlock the door and follow her inside.

As soon as the door shuts, she turns on me, arms

crossed over her chest. "Why are you being so weird and rude? You were glowering at Duke and his friends like you wanted to run them over with your truck. It was just a game. And I was winning. Why are you being all cranky again? Did I do something?"

"No. You didn't do anything wrong. It's just . . ." How can I explain? I slide my hands into my hair. "Duke wants you."

She blinks in surprise. "Duke? No. Well, maybe, but I think maybe he's like that with everyone."

How can she not see it? How can she be so blind? I move closer, shaking my head. "You're too naïve."

"I am not." Her chin lifts in defiance.

I hold up my hands. "Okay, so you're smart. Super smart. Probably the smartest person I've ever met. But you don't know anything about guys."

She bites her lip, drawing my gaze to her mouth. "I guess you're right. But that's why I have to learn."

"You want to learn?" I take another step toward her.

"I suppose," she says uncertainly, but she holds her ground and now we're scant inches apart.

"You want to learn with Duke?" I ask and hold my breath for her answer.

"I—" She cuts off with a frown. "No. I don't think so."

"Good." And then my hands do what I've been imagining for the past week and cup her delicate face as I lean in.

17

If you can be content right now, then you'll always be content, because it's always right now.

—Willie Nelson

Reese

I'm stuck. Frozen. Can't move. Can't speak. I can't believe Fitz is going to kiss me. For reals this time.

Wait. Is he? He's not quite there yet. He's in front of me, his hands on my jaw, his mouth nearly touching mine, our breathing labored and tangled in the space between us.

"Is it okay if I . . ." he asks.

There's a tremble in his voice, restraint in the hands cupping my face. He's not acting like some romance movie hero where the guy takes what he wants, kissing with force and strength like I might have expected but wouldn't have wanted. Not really.

Instead, he's gentle and waiting. Waiting for me.

Making the moment mine.

"Fitz." His name is a benediction on my lips and then I'm gripping his wrists, keeping his hands on me.

I sway forward, meeting him with a soft touch of my lips against his.

My first kiss.

And I took it.

Initially, a press of lips is all it is, just a hint of flesh, a gentle entreaty, a tentative meeting and introduction, *hi how are you*, but then the conversation gets deeper. I need to get closer. Engage in more meaningful discourse. I'm not sure who opens their mouth first, but we dive into a debate with tongues and lips and gentle sucks.

I never imagined, never understood. Heat floods through me, filling my center with throbbing need.

When he bites my bottom lip, I can't help the moan that emerges from somewhere deep inside, the sound foreign and unfamiliar. I can't believe I'm making these strange, needy noises, and they keep coming out.

Fitz lifts me easily, his hands strong and warm around my waist and then we're on the bed and he's over me. His eyes meet mine, searching, seeking approval and I give it readily. My hands wrap around his neck to keep his mouth on mine, and my legs fall open as he presses between them. My body knows exactly what it wants even if my mind isn't quite sure yet. Our mouths are fused, tongues exploring and tasting. I can't stop my body from responding, rubbing myself up against him, making him groan and press down harder.

"Yes," I say into his mouth.

Even though I've never been kissed till tonight, I know exactly what I'm feeling pressing against me, through his jeans, and I need *more*.

Pounding at the door makes both of us jump. "Hey, are you guys still playing? The game's starting again."

We stare at each other, breathless and panting. His eyes are dark and hooded and his lips are swollen.

"Be right there," Fitz calls out, his voice strangled.

Sound sifts back into my consciousness. There's still a party raging in the house and I'm in the room. With Fitz. And we nearly . . . well, not really *that*, but still. Didn't he disappear with Abby less than an hour ago?

Hesitation crosses his face and with a sudden movement that casts a breeze against my skin, he's backing off and lifting himself away.

He tunnels both hands through his hair and takes a deep breath before releasing his grasp.

"Reese, I didn't mean to—"

"It's okay. I mean, I did it. Not you."

"You didn't. I initiated it."

"And then I made it happen."

"But I let it get out of hand."

"Okay, so we're both in trouble."

He smiles, a lopsided twist of his mouth. The same mouth that was just over me, doing magical things to my lips and tongue I didn't even know were possible.

"It's just, is this a good idea? Right now? Us?" he asks.

The word *us* on his lips sends a sizzle down my spine and all the way to my toes. "I don't know. I mean, there's Abby to consider."

"There really isn't though."

"Maybe. But she was just here, and like it or not, she's still part of your life right now."

He opens his mouth like he wants to object, then stops. His eyes break away, and like an open sore, Abby festers between us.

"And then there's the whole fight to the death thing," I add.

He laughs and the tension eases somewhat. He shoves his hands in his pockets. "I don't care about Abby. I don't care much about the competition either. All I know is I would like there to be an us. But the truth is . . . the truth is I'm a bit scared."

"Scared? Of what?"

"Of you."

"Me?" I laugh. "I am not frightening."

"But you are. I guess I'm more scared of how I feel. If it's real, if I know what I want . . . All I know is I like you. And quite honestly, I'm not sure what to do about it."

"Does something need to be done?"

He takes a step closer, sitting on the foot of the bed. "Well, Reese, when you like someone, you typically, you know, date."

I'm blushing again. "I know that much."

"But it might be weird, us dating and all, given that we basically live together."

"For now."

"Right. For now. I guess the question is, how do *you* feel? About me, specifically."

"I'm not sure."

He nods. "I guess I understand. You've seen me at some not-so-fine moments. I think in most relationships, you only show the good stuff initially and not all the bad stuff right away. We kind of went the opposite way."

"It's not . . . I don't dislike you or anything. It's just, I'm scared too. I've never—as you know—had any kind of . . . anything. With anyone. It's terrifying."

"Terrifying? Not horrifying, though?"

I smile. "Frightening. Chilling. Daunting and intimidating."

"Is it less scary now that we've named it?"

"No. I think I'm just a scaredy-cat in general."

"I think you're pretty fierce, actually."

I laugh softly. "No one's ever attributed that adjective to me."

"I could come up with more." He leans closer and watches me. His eyes flicker to my mouth and then meet my eyes. "Tenacious. Intelligent. Kind. Passionate. Beautiful."

I shake my head, but no words come out. How do I respond?

"This doesn't have to be so complicated," he says. "We could be scared together."

"Fearful of each other but together." I laugh.

"Just . . . promise to tell me if you're thinking

anything weird or crazy and I'll do the same. And no other boys. No Dukes. And no Abbys."

"No Dukes. No Abbys. Got it. What about the competition?"

"I don't know. We still have two more challenges and at least four more days until Jude announces the winner. We can keep on as we have been. I'll even take the floor if you want. There are no obligations. And as far as what happens when this whole thing is over . . . we can jump off that bridge when we get to it."

"Which is ironic, since I might be living under an actual bridge."

"I won't let that happen." He reaches over and picks up my hand, lacing our fingers together.

My stomach flutters and I swallow past a suddenly dry mouth, my gaze focused on our hands. "What else would you suggest?"

"We could tell Jude we've decided to live here together, just share."

I look up. "You really think it's smart to live together so soon into our . . . whatever this is? It seems like a terrible decision."

"You're likely right." His hand squeezes mine. "Listen, don't worry about it. We'll figure it out. Annabel said she would look into something at the paper, and hey, maybe Granny will let me stay with her."

I laugh. "She probably would. But she really liked Beast. Maybe we can get him over there and I'll take his room."

"I dunno, he's pretty protective of Jude, and vice versa. I don't think they would leave each other."

"That's true." Our eyes meet and his gaze slips to my mouth.

I swallow and lick my lips and his hand tenses in mine.

"Well, don't think I'm letting you off easy for these events coming up," I say.

"I wouldn't dream of it," he says, just before his mouth captures mine.

18

ou don't love because: you love despite; not for the virtues, but despite the faults.

—William Faulkner

Fitz

Abby keeps calling, then when I don't answer, she moves to texting.

I read the first few. She's apologetic at first, then increasingly irate until I shut my phone off so I can focus on the here and now. I'm a little worried and a lot frustrated. Abby *seemed* sincere about wanting to be friends and giving me time, but she didn't mean it. I will not be manipulated. Not anymore.

Jude cooks dinner, then Reese and I do our homework at the dining table, exchanging secret smiles and amused glances every time Beast lumbers in to bring us a drink or a new pencil when the lead on mine snaps.

When it's time for bed, I wait until we've both brushed our teeth and Reese is setting up her blankets on the floor.

"Reese, I can't let you sleep on the floor."

She frowns at me. "Why not?"

"Sleep up here." I pat the mattress beside me. "With me."

She blinks rapidly. Her mouth opens. Then shuts. Then opens again.

"I mean just sleep. I would never pressure you into anything you didn't want to do. You trust me, right?"

"I do, it's just—" She bites her lip, not meeting my eyes. "I have flutters."

"Flutters?"

"Nerves. Bad ones. It's not like butterflies in the stomach. It's like a wandering albatross."

"An albatross, huh?" I fight to contain my laughter. "That bad?"

"They have the longest recorded wingspan."

"Really?" The laughter is under control but I can't stop the grinning.

"Twelve feet."

"That is bigger than butterflies. Why?"

"Why what?"

"Why are you nervous?" I keep my expression neutral.

She regards me for a few long seconds, and then finally it spills out. "What if I drool on you? What if I stink when I sleep? What if you wake up and look at me in the morning and realize it's all a mistake?"

"We have slept next to each other before and you didn't turn into an ogre overnight. Not that I remember."

"But still, what if there's . . ." Her hand flails for a second in frustration. "Flatulence."

I bark out a laugh, and then can't stop laughing. "Are you saying you might fart on me?"

Her face is now bright red. "See? I am no good at this."

"Actually, I think you're very, very good at this." I move away from the bed and take a step toward her, getting close enough so I can take both her hands and link her fingers with mine.

"Come to bed. With me. I promise I won't run out of here gagging if you fart all over me in your sleep." The words come out mixed with laughter.

"This isn't funny."

"It's a little funny. Unless you really don't want to. Then I wouldn't make you. If you would rather stay away from me, I won't cry too much."

She smiles, the movement small and shy. "It's not that I don't want to." She slides in the bed first, scooting toward the wall, on her side, facing me. I leave the lights on—maybe it will make her more comfortable if she can see—and slide in next to her and lie on my back, trying not to crowd her, but I take one hand and link our fingers, shutting my eyes.

Her hand clutches against mine, but tension vibrates off her.

I crack an eye open and find her staring at me, eyes wide in the dim light.

The chuckles can't be held back.

"Why are you laughing?" Her voice is indignant, but she's smiling.

"You look terrified. You can sleep. Do you want me to turn off the lights?"

"No. Maybe I like watching you sleep."

"That's worse than the farting, creeper."

"Stop it." She smacks me gently on the arm.

I lean over and kiss her on the lips, slowly, making sure she sees me coming and that she's okay with it. It's a small kiss, a light tap of lips and then I move back to lie on my side, facing her. The faint flush of her skin makes her radiant under the soft illumination.

After a few long seconds, she leans over and her mouth covers mine.

And so it goes. We face each other under the fairy lights and kiss for a while. Then we stop to gather ourselves and talk. And laugh. And the conversation turns into really random things. Mostly because I'm trying to calm the happy guy in my pants by thinking about bizarre topics unrelated to Reese's soft skin or the feel of her hands when she runs them under my shirt and up my back, casting chills over my body.

"Why do they sell hot dogs in packages of ten and buns in packages of eight?" I ask. "It just plain don't make sense."

She leans over and kisses me, then leans back with a smile. "The world is full of things that don't make sense."

"It really is, like, why do people give flowers to people for special occasions? I mean, it's kinda arbitrary. What's the point?"

She nods and tucks one hand under her head. I have her other hand in mine, our fingers playing and tracing and feeling. "Actually, the history of flower giving can be traced back to ancient Greece, when it was thought that flowers were associated with the gods. And in Turkey, they assigned meanings to different flowers, which then was adopted by Victorian culture as a part of the courting ritual. In Japan, it's called *hanakotoba*, where various plants are used for passwords and codes."

"Wow. Really? You seriously know everything." And then it's my turn to lean over and kiss her, on the mouth, slipping my tongue inside, tasting her smart words.

This distracts both of us for a few long seconds before Mr. Happy starts taking over my brain and I pull back again.

She resumes our conversation like it wasn't just interrupted. "I guess a plant or a flower in a pot might be better, since at least it has more of a shelf life. Why cut something that's alive, give it to a loved one, and then they watch while it dies? It's kinda morbid actually, if you think about it."

"What's your idea of the perfect gift, then?"

"Books," she answers without hesitation.

"Any old book will do?"

"Well . . . I collect first editions."

"Is that what the box was?" My eyes trail over to the

closet, where I helped her shove the small but heavy box onto the top shelf.

She sits up and scoots to the end of the bed, then over to the closet, reaching up to grab it. She's wearing flimsy sleep shorts, and when she reaches up, her shirt rides up and I get a peek of her pale stomach.

She has no idea how hot she is.

And I'm being a barbarian while she struggles and tugs.

Jumping up, I stand behind her and stretch overhead, pulling the box down and setting it on the foot of the bed.

She pulls the flaps open and hands me one from the top.

"*Northanger Abbey*," I read the title.

"It's not a first edition, but it's my favorite."

I turn it over in my hand. It's bound in red cloth with ornate gold decorations threaded into the cover. I open it gingerly. The pages are yellow and brittle with age.

"Why is this one your favorite?"

"It was Jane Austen's first book. Well, the first she finished for publication, although it wasn't actually published until after her death. It's also a comedy."

I meet her eyes. "Is it?"

"It's a satire of gothic novels, which were very popular during her life. And she did something unique for the period. Most of the sentimental novels of the time featured exceptionally beautiful heroines and heroes who fall madly in love with them. Jane reversed the gender stereotype by having the heroine Catherine fall for Henry first, and he isn't immediately attracted to her but falls eventually when they get to know each other."

"Sounds interesting, actually. So this isn't a first edition? It looks pretty old."

"No. I think maybe it's the first from this particular publisher though. It was printed in 1920." She turns the title page and points out the date on the reverse side. "The real British first edition is from 1818 and would be worth thousands. At least."

"Wow."

"You want to read it?"

"Really? Yeah. I do. If it's your favorite, it must be good. Although I'm disappointed you aren't a *Pride and Prejudice* fan. I was named after Mr. Darcy."

Her eyes light up. "Really?"

"My momma's a librarian."

"I love her already."

I laugh and her cheeks tint pink and we continue to look through her book stash.

She points out different titles along with various facts about each one and every time her face glows with delight, I fall a little more in love with her.

After a time, I put the box back in the closet—minus *Northanger Abbey*, which goes onto the bedside table—and we lie back down next to each other in the small bed.

"Are all of those books gifts from your parents?"

"No. I purchased most of them. I mean, with their money, so in a sense I suppose they are from them. But they don't really give gifts. The only person who's given me anything nonessential is my sister."

"Your parents don't buy you birthday or Christmas presents?"

"Not really. They don't celebrate those things."

"Oh. Because of their religion? Are they Jehovah's Witnesses?"

"Granny is religious—she's Baptist—but my parents are anything but. Honestly, I think they forget. They're not home much and they tend to be real absorbed in their own lives. They aren't bad people. They always made sure we were taken care of, had food and shelter, and whatever necessities or things we wanted whenever we wanted. It's not like I ever went without."

"Huh. I can't imagine. We didn't have a lot of money, growing up, but Christmas and birthdays were always a big deal. My mom would go all out. Special dinner and presents I had been waiting to get for months. I can't imagine getting what I want whenever I want it. On the surface it sounds great, but the reality seems . . . kinda sad, actually. Half the fun of Christmas morning was the anticipation of getting something you'd been wanting forever."

She's silent again, and this time, her eyes are shut. Is she sleeping? But then she speaks. "I wish I could have a Christmas like that."

"I'm sure you will. You're still young. Now you get to find and make your own family. If that's what you want, I mean."

"Right," she says, the word quiet in the dim room.

"What kind of present would you ask for? From Santa."

"Hmmm. I don't know. Probably not flowers. Something useful, maybe?"

"Like a survival pack? Full of bandages and Spam?"

She laughs. "Other canned goods might be preferable."

I run a hand up her arm to her shoulder, tracing the lines of her, memorizing her with my fingertips, and she smiles at me.

"Is this what it's always like?"

"What do you mean?"

"When you're with someone. This . . . talking, kissing, laughing, and nothing more. Is it normal?"

I prop my head up on one hand. "I dunno. I never did much of this with Abby. She was more into going out, being seen. And when we had conversations, it was mostly surface stuff. Or she would talk about herself, how she felt about others." I frown. "It was always about her."

She mimics my position so we're eye to eye. "That sounds like her. So instead of talking you . . . just did other stuff?"

I know what she means by "other stuff." I watch her face. Is she worried I'm not attracted to her?

"Abby and I didn't have a huge physical relationship. I mean, we did *other stuff*, but not as much as you might think. She was busy doing *other stuff* with other people." I reach out and trail a line down her jaw. "With you, it's different. It's not that I don't want to do the other stuff with you. Clearly." I gesture to the semi in my lap that won't quit. "But this is good. This is more than enjoyable. For me."

"Really?"

"Reese." I cup her face in my hands, tracing her cheekbones with my thumbs. "I'm all in. Considering our past relationships, or lack thereof, I think it's probably smart to go slow. And this is . . . nice. This is more than nice."

Her responding smile is brilliant. "It is. But let's not take too long on the rest."

19

If you can't do it with feeling, don't.
—Patsy Cline

REESE

"WE ARE STEPPING THINGS UP HERE, BABIES. OBSTACLE course under duress! There's only two more Bedlam events and the score is three to two with Fitz Moreland in the lead!"

Scattered applause.

"Our audience gets to participate in the fun tonight. As you can see, we have an obstacle course of sorts set up here."

It's relatively unchanged from the setup for laser tag—everything has just been rearranged. And now there are two welcome mats set up next to each other. In front of the mats is a path of old tires that leads to a ramp, which leads to some kind of downward zip line through the yard. After that await two kiddie pools—one for each of us—filled with mud and some kind of stepping stones set up inside. Then a climbing wall at the end.

It doesn't look too hard, actually.

"Not only do you have to get through the course, you have to do it all while keeping your egg safe." He holds up two eggs. "And to make it even more exciting." Jude holds up two pairs of shoes.

Not regular shoes. Heels.

I groan and Fitz laughs.

"To make it fun for you babies," he yells over the crowd, "you all get water balloons to throw at our competitors."

Beast carries out two giant buckets, which I presume contain the balloons.

"Are you kidding me?" I ask.

Fitz, meanwhile, is rubbing his hands together. "This is gonna be awesome."

"Reese, Fitz, your goal is to get to the end first without breaking your egg. If you break your egg at any point, you're out."

"What if both of our eggs break?" I ask.

"Then you try again until someone finishes with their egg intact."

He hands us our shoes, and I can't help but laugh when Fitz does a little jig and then struts by me on the grass like it's a catwalk.

"How are you so good at that?" I nearly trip over the welcome mat just standing up.

"I'll never tell you my secrets," he sasses me, hands on his hips.

Still laughing, we line up on our mats and then Jude gives the countdown. "On your mark. Get set. Go!" He blows the horn.

And we're off. Fitz is like lightning in heels while I struggle to get through the tires without falling on my face or breaking my egg. Finally, I stick it in my sports bra top and haul ass, running over the ramp. There are water balloons flying everywhere. They break apart at my feet, nearly tripping me, and then one smacks my shoulder with a sharp bite. The water is *cold*. It's a good thing the night still carries the heat from the day.

I glance over at Fitz and he's getting hit way worse.

When I risk a glance at the crowd, I can see why. Annabel has recruited people to hit him harder—I guess it is good having her in my corner.

I make it down the short zip line. One balloon narrowly misses my head, making me laugh with unrestrained mirth. I've never had such a great time.

I make it through the kiddie pool without further mishap, but Fitz is on the climbing wall already.

Jumping up after him, I scramble to the top, but he gets there before me with a foot to spare.

But when I get next to him, he opens his hand and reveals his broken, runny egg.

Jude meets us at the top, climbing up a set of stairs in the back of the wall.

He tsks at Fitz's egg. "Humpty Dumpty'ed it. Too bad. Reese? Your egg?"

I reach into my bra and Fitz's eyes widen and then heat. Not removing my gaze from his, I hold up my unbroken egg with a smile.

"Reese Jackson has won this round, babies!" Jude lifts my hand in the air and pulls the key from around his neck, sliding it over my head.

The expected groans and cheers emanate from the crowd, but I can't take my eyes off Fitz. He's still watching me, eyes dark and intent. He hasn't so much as glanced away ever since I pulled the egg from my bra. His shirt is wet and molded to his body like a second skin.

Fitz circles round Jude, grabs my hand and then we're heading down the stairs.

"Where are we going?" I ask him, breathless and shivering from the wet clothes sticking to my skin.

"To get dried off."

We have to navigate through the crowd and deal with people trying to talk to us, but Fitz cuts through them like a man on a mission. Once we're at the door to the room, I unlock it with the key and immediately kick off the heels digging into my feet while he grabs dry clothes.

His phone is on the dresser and it lights up with a buzz. He grimaces at it before shutting it off and tossing it back down. Then his eyes are on me again. "Shower?" he asks.

I nod, still shivering. "Yes, please."

We lock it up and head to the bathroom together, pushing through people and cutting through the line.

He shuts and locks the door behind us and turns to me, his back resting against the door.

He's still in the heels.

"You've got experience wearing high heels?"

"I have an older sister." He shrugs and steps away from the door, moving closer. "We played dress up."

I laugh. "Seriously?"

He takes another step toward me. "If you repeat this to anyone, I'll tell them about your flatulence problem."

And then we're laughing and his hand is on my shoulder and we're still laughing as our lips come together. At first soft and tentative and limned with mirth, but then morphing and coalescing into something harder and faster.

His mouth is hot and insistent but his hands are gentle when they start to tug my wet shirt over my head.

"Is this okay?" he asks.

"Yes." My voice is a breathy whisper that I don't recognize.

Then my shirt is gone and I'm standing in front of him in a wet pink sports bra. "Damn, Reese. You are so . . ." And then I miss the rest of whatever he says because his mouth covers mine again before his lips move, trailing a line down my neck. He stops to nip and lick at my collarbone before descending farther.

Heat sinks its tendrils into my skin everywhere his mouth touches. I grip his shoulders, unsure what to do with my hands, unsure what to do with anything.

Then his finger is pulling down the fabric of my bra and his mouth covers one nipple while his hand covers the other. My mind goes completely blank and I can't see or think straight through all of the sensations flooding me. I think I'm making strangled sounds, but I can't be sure until he lifts his head to meet my eyes and I know he's checking on me.

"Don't stop," I say.

His answering grin is slow and satisfied and he yanks his shirt over his head, exposing an acre of golden-tanned male flesh that I devour with my gaze.

"Sweetheart, we're just getting started."

His naked skin is so close and so intriguing and I wonder if it will feel as good to him, what he did to me, and before I can second-guess myself, I run my hands down his chest and lean forward to put my mouth on his flat nipple.

A ragged sound emerges from somewhere deep in his chest. He hisses through his teeth, tugging me away, watching me with hooded eyes before our mouths clash together again and our chests meet, skin on skin, lips searching, learning, sucking.

I yank at his pants blindly, struggling with the wet fabric until he pulls back so we can toss the rest of our soaked clothes into a heap on the floor.

Fitz reaches into the shower and turns the handle, his hand cupping the side of my neck, and then his mouth comes back, meeting mine. The room fills with the thrum of water, drowning out the music and voices from outside our little cocoon of slow-moving steam.

Then we're in the small shower, my back against the cold tile and his under the stream of hot water. Rivets slide down his golden skin, pulled tight over lean muscle. My hands trace the path the water takes until I reach his hips and stare down at his rock-hard member, larger than I expected, both intriguing and slightly terrifying.

I start to wonder what I'm supposed to do with this thing, exactly. I mean, I understand the mechanics but I've never—

And then all those thoughts slip away as his hands slide over my curves down and down and down.

His fingers dip between my legs, pressing and luring and coaxing sensation. And then all I can do is feel. His dark eyes flash, intense and focused, while his hand makes me twist and buck and keen. I clutch at him, grabbing his shoulders to keep from forming a puddle of limbs at his feet.

His mouth moves back to my breast, tongue laving at my nipple. His free hand goes to my other breast, and I jerk against his hand between my legs. His fingers falter for a moment and then move again, caressing with the flat of his palm *right there* where I need it. A finger slides into me and I break, biting my lip to hold back the flood of sound threatening to fly out of my lips.

The water patters against the tile, tugging me back into consciousness. I open my eyes and find Fitz watching me, his eyes hooded, his mouth parted and swollen.

He grasps his erection with the same hand that just pleasured me, sliding it back and forth.

My body is still quivering from the most intense

orgasm of my life, and I stare at his movements, watching him pleasure himself in fascination. Up and down. I'd rather like to touch him that way myself. Inexplicably, heat begins to fill my stomach again. I never thought I would find such a sight erotic, but it absolutely is. Or maybe it's just him.

I slip one hand down and over his fingers and move with him. Feeling the movement kicks everything up a notch, sending heat swirling into my stomach.

After a minute, he lets go, leaning both arms on either side of my head against the cool tile at my back and we both watch as I imitate his prior movements. Back and forth, experimenting with the flesh in my hand that's like hard steel under soft skin.

A gentle stroke. Then a little harder. Slower. Then faster. I catalogue his reactions, noting which ones have a higher value and making sure to repeat those with greater frequency. There's an order of importance—when he bites his lip, when his breathing falters, when his eyes fall shut, and especially when he groans out loud.

"Reese, I can't . . ." His shoulders shake and his entire body shudders. His eyes squeeze shut, mouth twisted in pleasure, and I watch in fascination as he erupts all over my stomach.

He leans forward, resting his head on my shoulder while his breathing eases and the shower washes away the evidence of our time together.

I trace the muscles in his back. "That was . . ." For the first time, I don't have any words.

He pulls his head back, meeting my eyes. "I hope you're about to say something synonymous with good. Or maybe great? Stupendous?"

I laugh. "Something along those lines. And enlightening. Educational."

"If you need to do any more learning, I'm available to provide instruction."

"Good to know."

We share a laugh and then the water temperature drops by ten degrees.

Fitz grimaces and shuts the tap off. "I guess we've been in here awhile."

He steps out of the shower and hands me a clean towel from the rack. "Here."

A banging on the door makes me jump.

"Fitz! Are you in there?" Annabel's voice is high and strained.

"Yeah." His startled eyes meet mine and the toweling ceases. "What's going on? Is it Dad?"

"No. Not Dad." She stops and the sound of people laughing and the hum of the crowd fills the space. Then she speaks again. "It's Abby. She's in the hospital."

20

I'm a Texas guy, and the good and bad of that is that I'm always, first and foremost, loyal.

—Jared Padalecki

Fitz

I SCRAMBLE TO COVER UP, WRAPPING THE TOWEL AROUND my waist. Reese stays hidden behind the door while I crack it open.

"What happened?"

"I don't know. Momma didn't say much. She's on her way to the hospital to be with Abby's parents. All I know is it was some kind of car accident. She said she's been trying to call you. They've all been trying to see if you knew what was going on."

Abby called me. Right before we showered and I

ignored it. How could I have discerned her normal attention-seeking behavior from a real emergency? "Is she okay?"

"I don't know. You gotta come though. Sorry, Reese."

Reese makes a sound of assent and understanding, still hiding behind the door in nothing but a towel. Though she's biting her lip, expression worried.

"I'll be right out," I tell Annabel.

"I'll pull my car out front. Hurry."

I shut the door and immediately turn and take Reese in my arms.

This is not how I pictured the rest of this night going.

"I hope she's okay," Reese whispers into my neck.

"Me too."

"I feel . . . awful. I never liked her."

"Hey." I pull back and cup her face in both hands. "It's going to be okay. You didn't do anything wrong."

"But, Fitz, why were they trying to reach you for information? Why wouldn't they try Kevin? That's probably who she was with."

I realize suddenly I never told her everything. She has no idea I've been hiding the truth from my parents. But there's no time.

"It's a long story. I promise to explain everything later." I let her go and I'm already rushing, pulling on dry pants, yanking a T-shirt on. I don't know what to think or feel right now. Was this my fault? Would this have happened if I had answered her calls? "I'll call you when I get there and find out what's going on."

She nods and I give her one quick, gentle kiss, first on

the crease between her eyes and then a longer, more lingering one on her lips before leaving the bathroom.

I weave my way quickly through the busy house and out front, where Annabel's parked her car.

We're both silent, driving through the darkened, mostly empty streets of Blue Falls, toward the hospital. What if this time, the one time I didn't respond, Abby actually hurt herself? It would be all my fault. But that can't be it. She was going to get help. It's probably exactly what it sounds like—a simple car accident. Accident. Even the word implies no one's at fault.

It isn't until we're halfway there that Annabel speaks.

"What are you going to tell all the parents? They don't know you aren't together. Does Reese know they don't know?"

Guilt, already a razor-sharp companion, stabs through me, pricking at my skin like an aggravated porcupine. I should have told them a long time ago. All this protecting of Abby hasn't done her any favors. And I should have told Reese the whole story. I will, though, as soon as I can.

But first things first.

"I can't tell them yet." Not if what I suspect about this car accident is true, but I shove that thought away.

She sighs. "You have to tell them."

"I will tell them, eventually. Just not yet. What am I supposed to say? 'Hey, sorry your daughter nearly died and is in critical condition. By the way, we've been over for months and oh yeah she's been lying to you'?"

"I know it won't be a June picnic but don't you think

it's going to be worse if you keep it a secret and it comes out later?"

"No. I don't."

We get to the hospital and Annabel and I head to the emergency department.

The waiting room is mostly empty. An older man is being interviewed at a counter, and over in the corner, a young woman weeps quietly while another holds her hand.

Momma stands off to the side. She's alone.

She hugs us both.

"What happened?" I ask.

Before she can answer, the door to the emergency department swings open and Abby's parents emerge.

"Any news?" Momma asks them while Martha hugs Annabel and me in turn and Tom shakes my hand.

"She's okay. Not making much sense at the moment but that's because she has a concussion and her face is a bit bruised from the airbag so it's hard for her to speak. They're keeping her overnight for observation. She also has a bunch of scrapes and bruises, but otherwise . . ." Martha breaks off and starts crying softly. Her husband puts an arm around her shoulders and she turns into him, wilting against him like a deflating balloon.

Mr. Summers continues. "She's lucky. It would have been worse. She crashed into a tree. The officer at the scene said they don't think it was an accident." His voice is gruff.

"What does that mean?" Momma asks. "How could it not be an accident?"

"There weren't any brake marks. She wasn't veering away or trying to avoid crashing. And they did a blood test and a tox screen. She wasn't on anything."

"What are you saying, Tom?" Momma's eyes are wide. "She crashed on purpose?"

Mr. Summers meets my eyes, his own grave and intense.

The waiting room falls away as shock rolls through me. A tidal wave of guilt and shame floods over me, the feeling so visceral it roars in my ears.

She *did* hurt herself intentionally. I didn't want to believe it, not after everything . . .

I blink Mr. Summers into focus, realizing he's speaking to me, asking me something.

"Has she said anything to you? Do you know where she was going or what she was doing? We looked through her phone. She had been calling you a lot but it doesn't look like you were answering."

His tone isn't censorious, but there's an unspoken question in his words.

Why weren't you with her?

"The truth is, sir . . ."

Martha sniffs and meets my eyes, her own red rimmed and tired.

"My phone broke. I dropped it when I was running yesterday and I haven't had it replaced. I had no idea anything was wrong. I haven't talked to Abby in a couple days. School has been . . . busy."

The excuses are lame, even to my own ears, but no one notices.

Except Annabel, who is still standing out of sight of everyone else. She just rolls her eyes.

Martha reaches for me, taking my hand in hers and squeezing. "They're moving her upstairs to a room shortly. I'm sure she's going to want to see you."

I squeeze her hand back, unsure how to respond. I hate everything about this.

"I want to see her too."

EXCEPT I DON'T END UP SEEING ABBY UNTIL MORNING. BY the time they move her to a room for the night, it's nearly midnight and visiting hours are way over.

So I do what any person pretending to be someone's long-time boyfriend would do: I stay the night. All night. Dozing in an uncomfortable chair and thinking too much about Abby and her parents—who also stay the night, except Martha stays in Abby's room—and wondering how the heck all of this is going to shake out and how much trouble I'm gonna gather along the way.

Annabel and Momma leave, promising to return in the morning.

It's a little after seven when I finally get the okay to go to Abby's room. At first, I think I'm not gonna get a chance to talk to her about anything important because her momma's still there.

This is gonna be bizarre as hell, pretending to be her boyfriend when it's so over.

But the moment I see Abby, take in her bruised and

battered face, dark and swollen, none of that matters. I take her hand. Lean forward and kiss her head. I would've done that anyway. Despite our past, Abby is still an old friend.

"Can you talk?" I ask in a hushed tone.

"A little." Her lip is swollen, her voice low but steady.

"I'll go get some coffee. Give you two a minute." Martha pats our joined hands before heading out the door.

As soon as she's out, Abby squeezes my hand. "You didn't tell them."

"No."

Her eyes shut in relief. "Thank you."

"I'm sorry you're hurting. I'm glad you're okay. What happened?"

She grimaces in pain. "I can't talk about it."

"Okay. Fine, I get it. But . . . I need to talk to you about your parents. We have to tell them the truth."

Her head shakes and her eyes are filling with tears. "No, Fitz, please. Give me a little more time."

"Abby, you need to talk to someone about all of this. Your parents can get you help. They love you, they want what's best for you."

One of her monitors beeps but the numbers mean nothing to me. Abby starts to shake and cry, tears falling freely down her face. This isn't manipulation, not anymore. She really looks like hell warmed over.

"Okay, okay," I relent. "You don't have to say anything yet. But Abby . . ."

I'm going to convince her to come clean soon, but how can I when she's in this condition?

"It's fine," I say and she finally starts to calm down a little. "It's all going to be fine."

I really hope I'm telling the truth.

21

The truth does not change according to our ability to stomach it.

—Flannery O'Connor

Reese

When my phone rings on Saturday midmorning, my heart leaps. Fitz!

But it's not Fitz.

"Annabel?"

"Hey, I wanted to let you know everything is okay. Abby is okay."

"I'm glad." I am, but I'm more concerned with someone else. "How's Fitz?"

"He's fine. Everyone's tired and hungry, I think.

Hospital food is terrible. They think she's gonna be released later tonight."

"That's good. What happened?"

"She crashed her car."

"Oh no," I breathe.

"We aren't sure exactly how it happened, but the cops think she intentionally drove off the road."

Guilt swamps me.

I knew Abby had problems, and now that I think back, they're smacking me right in the face and a few times upside the head for good measure.

The manic episodes, the neediness, the depression . . . the constant desire to take out her insecurities and problems on me as the nearest and most convenient punching bag.

I want to ask more about Fitz but I don't want to appear like the lovelorn weirdo I am.

Thankfully, Annabel answers my unspoken question.

"Fitz will probably stay here today and maybe at home or at Abby's parents' house tonight."

"Oh, okay."

He's going to stay with Abby? With her parents? That doesn't really make sense. I get that they're family friends and all, but does he really need to be with her this whole time? Doesn't she have Kevin? Isn't it odd since they broke up, over a month ago now? And Fitz has made it abundantly clear he needs distance from her.

"Listen, Reese . . . it's just that . . ." Annabel heaves a sigh and then her voice goes abrupt. "I gotta go. I'll call you later."

We hang up and I'm more confused than ever.

An anxious energy vibrates through me. I hate this waiting, uncertainty, not knowing. I want to do something. I hate sitting here, helpless.

Annabel did mention how terrible the food was. Maybe I can do something for them. Would it be weird to bring them homemade food? No. Couldn't be. This is the South, it's what we do—bring people food as a way to express sympathy. A time-honored tradition. Things always look better on a full stomach.

Plus it's what I've promised myself. I'm not going to run and hide from life. Not anymore.

I pick up my phone and call home. "Granny? Get the smoker ready."

A FEW HOURS LATER, I'VE PACKED BRISKET AND CORNBREAD and potatoes and collard greens into various disposable containers and I'm pulling into the hospital.

I carry the bags inside. God, I hope someone else hasn't already thought to bring them food. Though it's all I can do to convince myself anyone would be thankful for some homemade cooking.

The waiting room is nearly empty, and a kindly older nurse tells me Abby's family went home to get her a change of clothes and some incidentals and would I like to go visit Abby?

"There's a mini fridge in the room you can store the food in and Abby will likely enjoy some company."

I agree and she gives me the room number and directions to the nearest set of elevators.

My stomach flutters with nerves. Will Fitz be up there? Am I intruding? Maybe I will leave the food and go.

I find Abby's room with relative ease and I'm surprised to find she's alone, sleeping. Her eyes are shut, both of them dark with purple bruises. She looks so frail and tiny in the bed. It's such a stark contrast to the seemingly indestructible, imposing figure I used to live with.

I stand there for a few seconds, wondering what I should do. It's like I've reverted to the old Reese, awkward, fumbling, insecure. I straighten and make a decision. I'll put the food in the fridge, leave a note, and get out of here.

I'm quietly shutting the fridge door when there's a rustling from the bed.

"What are you doing here?" Abby's voice is low and gravelly.

I spin around as if caught with my hand in the cookie jar. "I was . . . bringing y'all some barbeque. Annabel told me the food is terrible, and Granny always says there ain't nothing that can't be fixed with some good grub or a little moonshine." I laugh to cover the fact that I'm so uncomfortable. My palms are sweating and I clutch them together in front of me.

"Aw. That's mighty kind of you, but Fitz already got us some food earlier."

"Oh."

She glances at the doorway and then motions for me

to come closer. When I step toward the bed, she lowers her voice like she's telling me a secret. "I should probably tell you so you don't embarrass yourself. Fitz and I are back together."

I'm not surprised by this statement. Not because I believe her, but because I know Abby and I know how easily she lies. It's all a game and she's the one with the controller. "Oh?" I say, keeping my tone carefully neutral.

"You don't believe me?"

"I didn't say that."

I think she's smiling, but it's hard to tell because it looks sort of like a grimace with her face all swollen. "You think you know everything. So smart, so clever. You don't know the half of it." Her tone is laced with superiority. "I knew all it would take was a little scare to get Fitz back. He's gonna be so worried about me and what I'll do next, he won't leave my side."

The floor drops out from under me. Is she suggesting that she *did* intentionally drive off the road, but the ultimate goal wasn't to harm herself, but to get Fitz back?

"That would be quite a risk," I say carefully. "Running off the road. How did you know you wouldn't get hurt worse?"

She waves a hand. "The shoulder was a little steeper than I anticipated. But it all worked out for the best."

I don't know what to say or how to respond. And it doesn't matter because a middle-aged woman enters the room.

"You're awake!" She's more petite than Abby, but they have the same blonde hair and blue eyes. "And you have a visitor." Her smile is wide. "Hello, I'm Abby's momma, Martha."

"Nice to meet you."

We shake hands across Abby's bed.

This moment is so surreal, I can't believe I'm in a hospital meeting Abby's momma while she lies between us, her last words hanging over my head like a dialogue box in a comic strip.

"Did you and Abby meet at school?" she asks.

I glance down at Abby, my tongue stuck in my mouth while she somehow manages to look smug despite the bruised face. I swallow and find my words. "We did. We used to live in the dorms together."

Her head tilts at me, her brow creasing in confusion. "Used to?"

"Momma, Reese brought us some homemade barbeque. She put it in the fridge," Abby interjects.

"Well, aren't you sweet. Abby, you never told me about your roommate."

"We don't hang much," Abby says. "We both stay busy with school. And I have track too, and any spare time is spent with Fitz, you know."

"Oh, don't I know it." Abby's momma laughs, and she tells me, "You know, they've been like two peas in the same pod ever since they were kids."

I blink. "Yes. I know."

I do know, but the way she's speaking, it's like they really haven't broken up.

Uncertainty flickers through me. What if Abby's plan

worked? What if he is back with her? If only to save her from herself.

There's a sound from the doorway and Martha turns around. "Speaking of the devil. We were just talking about you. Did you get everything you needed from home?"

"Hey, baby." Abby's voice is warm and smug, her eyes boring into me.

My own gaze is fixed to the back of Martha's head, where her hair has been pulled back into a perfect bun.

Heart pounding, I finally look at the doorway. My heart lifts at the sight of him, and I could swear his own face brightens for a second when his eyes meet mine, but then his expression turns to one of horror.

I don't think it's because he's scruffy and tired and worn as an old shoe and hates for me to see him like this.

He blankets his expression quickly, but it's too late.

His eyes flick from Abby and her momma back to me.

"Yeah, I got my stuff." He lifts the bag he's carrying. An overnight bag. Because he's staying here . . . with her?

"Hey, Reese." His eyes shift away.

"Reese was kind enough to bring us some food for later, baby," Abby says to him.

His Adam's apple bobs when she calls him baby, and I can't move. What do I say to that?

Clearly, they are back together.

"Fitzy, why are you still standing there?" Abby laughs. "Why don't you put the bag under the bed over here and come give me a kiss now that I can feel my lips again?"

I can't.

My throat closes up in distress.

I can't stand here and watch them hug and kiss and act like a couple.

"It was nice to meet y'all." I keep my eyes on Abby's momma. "I . . . have somewhere I have to be."

I smile at Mrs. Summers and ignore the rest of the room in an awkward move worthy of every bad thing anyone's ever thought about me.

Then I bail, striding past Fitz without looking back. I don't have to. I can feel all the eyes on me.

Once I'm out the door, I have to stop for a second and lean back against the wall to catch my breath.

"She's . . . a strange duck," Abby's momma says.

Her tone isn't malicious, and she's not wrong, but the words sting anyway.

I don't stick around to hear Abby's response. Or Fitz's, for that matter, if there is one.

I walk. And then I keep walking. The hospital is a blur of people and white corridors. I have to get out of here, but I'm so discombobulated that I end up lost.

Finally, a kind nurse directs me to the nearest exit and I make my way outside.

I'm halfway to my car before I notice him. He's already there, leaning against the driver's side door, hands stuffed in his pockets. I stop and glance back at the hospital—is it too late to go hide in a bathroom?

"Reese." He steps away from the car.

As he approaches, I studiously ignore the attractive way he moves, the confidence of his gait, the lean muscles in his arms flexing. I wrap my arms around my middle. "You know, Abby didn't really try to hurt herself. Well, she did, but not to actually inflict damage."

He stops a few feet in front of me. "What are you talking about?"

"She told me she did it to get your attention."

His mouth opens, then closes.

"But it doesn't matter, does it? You're still with her."

"No. No, I'm not."

"Her momma thinks you are."

He grimaces. Shoving his hands in his pockets, his head falling back and his eyes shutting for a brief moment before he gives me one quick nod. "Yes."

"Does your family know?"

"We didn't tell our parents about the breakup. I told Abby I would wait. She was already in trouble for other stuff and I figured we could tell them later."

"So that's the real reason you couldn't live with your parents. You didn't want her to get in trouble. You were protecting her."

"Initially, yes. But then my parents decided to sell and move anyway, so it wouldn't have mattered."

"When are you gonna tell them?"

His eyes are dark with concern. "I'm not sure."

I stare down at the street, where a dandelion has had the audacity to take root in a crack of asphalt. Somehow, this little weed was strong enough to grow in the least hospitable environment. I'm sure there's a metaphor somewhere in there but my heart is hurting so badly it's affecting my brain, and nothing is coming to mind except wanting to be somewhere else. Anywhere else. Away from all this.

"Even now? After what I just told you? It's one thing for Abby to be a drama queen, it's quite another to . . . to lie and pretend she's suicidal with the sole purpose of messing with your life. Can't you see that?"

"I can't—I don't know. I need to think about it."

"It's not like I want to meet your parents as your girlfriend or anything yet anyway. But . . . Fitz. It hurts that you don't care enough to tell people we're together. Because . . . we are? Aren't we? I didn't mistake everything that's been happening, did I?"

"You didn't. It's just not a good time."

"Right." I nod. "I understand. I really do. It's just that . . . I deserve better."

He takes a step closer but I dance back.

He freezes and blinks. Something heavy moves behind his eyes. "You do. You do deserve better."

The words aren't unkind but they still hurt like a blade. "I've got to go."

I step around him and he doesn't stop me.

22

This idea that we are our own saviors, our own heroes. That's hard, but also incredibly uplifting.

—Reese Witherspoon

Reese

The drive to Jude's is a blur. I shouldn't have looked back when I was leaving Fitz, but I did. I watched him in my rear view, his hands clenched in his hair while he crouched on the ground. Did his heart hurt like mine?

But he broke it.

It's all his choice.

Yes, Abby is bruised and hurting, but she did it all to herself, and she's pretending to be suicidal for sympathy and to manipulate Fitz. It's a horrible, no good, terrible thing to do.

The realization doesn't make me feel any better, only worse.

When I get to Jude's, I immediately realize I can't stay here. I can't handle being in the room where we were so close, in the shower where he made me feel like a goddess.

I don't feel worshipped now, I'm more . . . wrung out to dry. Discarded like four-day-old casserole.

There's a physical ache in my body and this place doesn't help. It's just a reminder of being judged and decreed not good enough.

What if I'm never enough?

I pack my clothes and my most important box of books and get in the car to drive home.

The sun is setting as I head down Main Street. I pass the Frostee Freeze where Fynn and I had sundaes with Jude a few days ago. Ol' Roy is at the H-E-B. I don't bother waving this time.

I pull up in the drive on a cloud of dust.

The porch lights are on and Granny's out front. With the shotgun set over her lap. Again.

"Do you sit out here waiting for me to show up?" I call while I'm walking up to the porch.

She spits something off into the side yard. She must be feeling ornery if she's chewing tobacco. This doesn't bode well for me.

"That jackrabbit's out here again and he brought his friends. They've been pooping all over my flowers.

You showing up is a coincidence. Lucky timing, I suppose."

I walk up the steps. "I'm staying here tonight." My voice doesn't even waver.

She watches me with inscrutable eyes.

"You're not gonna shoot me," I say, straightening my spine and lifting my chin, like it might help.

She gets all squinty eyed, her lips pursed. "You sure about that, Tootsie Roll?"

I sigh and cross my arms over my chest. "If you're intending to do it, get it over with quick then."

There's a long pause, but the gun doesn't shift from where she's holding it over her lap, so that's something. "Good," she says finally. "You aren't scared anymore."

I stomp onto the patio in front of her, simultaneously frustrated and surprised by her words. Everything I've felt and thought since leaving Fitz behind at the hospital compresses into a ball in my stomach and explodes like the big bang.

"Are you kidding me? I'm scared to death. Of everything. Of what I feel, of what others think, of getting hurt, of making bad decisions, of things I've done—if they were worth it or if it will end in heartache and regret. And it's too late anyway because it already has. I've been trying. Talking to people, letting them in, allowing people to get close . . . and it hurts, Granny." My face crumples and I cover it for a moment, collecting myself before continuing. "And it's only going to get worse. I put myself out there and it was all for nothing. I'm worse off than I was."

She shakes her head and laughs at me.

Laughs. She laughs at me!

"Living is painful sometimes, Tootsie Roll. And you're being melodramatic. I'm glad though, it's about time. You're always too safe and serious. You upset about one of those fellas who came over for supper? Maybe the big guy?"

"Yes. And no, not the big guy. The other one. Fitz."

Granny nods. "Here." She leans down and grabs a mason jar from under the chair. "Have some moonshine."

"That's not going to help anything."

"Well, it ain't gonna hurt nothing either unless you drink too much. But it's like I always say. Life should be full of moon words. Moonlight kisses and moonshine and your ol' grandpappy mooning me from the front yard." She holds the mason jar higher, extending it toward me.

I snort out a laugh before taking the proffered drink and sitting in the chair next to her.

Then she hands me the other shotgun from under the seat.

I sit it across my lap, pointed out toward the side yard, so I can take a drink of the moonshine.

"I know you're unhappy, but things are better for you now." She puts a hand on my knee, shaking it briefly. "Doesn't matter what happens with that fella."

"I guess."

"Don't you give me that offhand baloney. It's about more than romance. You have friends. You're living your life instead of going through the motions and hiding yourself from the world."

"It's just . . . I'm not sure it's worth the risk."

"Oh, sugar, it's always worth the risk. Your grand-pappy has been dead for twenty years and even though I've now had more time without him than I had with him, and even though sometimes he made me madder than a spitting hen, I would do it all over again. Even knowing the pain. One second of happiness is better than nothing at all."

The moonshine slides down my throat with a harsh burn. A familiar-enough sensation and yet it never really softens. I pass the glass back to her.

"I was so worried about you, and now I'm not. You know why? You've always had a way of pulling into yourself, hiding from everything. I kept thinkin' it would get better over time, but it never did. Then when you got kicked outta the dorm and tried to come home, that's when I knew I had to take drastic measures. I had to put you out there, Tootsie Roll. You were scared you would fall, when I've always known you would fly. And see? I was right."

I sniff. "But I'm not flying. I'm falling. Crashing. None of this is better."

"Why did you run away when I had the shotgun the other week?" she asks abruptly.

"Uh, because you threatened to shoot me."

"And?"

"And . . . I was scared."

"What was the difference today? Were you not scared anymore?"

"No, I was still scared."

"But you did it anyway. With the fear. And things worked out fine. Life's like that sometimes. We're all scared. Be afraid. Then do it anyway. And Reese, baby, that's what you've been doing."

Her words hit me right in the gut. "Wow."

This might actually be the most profound thing I've ever heard Granny say, and she says a lot of stuff.

"That's right." She nods. "Sometimes you gotta take the skittles with the beer."

Aaand she's back.

A chuckle bubbles out of me. "That makes no sense, Granny."

"It does if you hate Skittles."

"Or beer." I smile.

She frowns. "No one hates beer."

I laugh so hard it brings tears to my eyes.

My laughter subsides and we're quiet again, waiting for the jackrabbits and passing the moonshine back and forth.

"Forget about this boy. If he doesn't see you for the prize you are, then he's as useless as a fart in a fan factory."

"Maybe it's the moonshine talking, but I think you're a genius."

23

Stand for something or you will fall for anything. Today's mighty oak is yesterday's nut that held its ground.

—Rosa Parks

Fitz

Thump. Thump. Thump.

"Fitz! Will you bring me some water? My throat is so dry."

Only a day has passed since I last saw Reese. Or spoke with her. But it's been a long day. A lifetime. I've called multiple times, but her phone always goes to voice mail. I tried texting too, but no response. I even tried to enlist Annabel to track her down, but she didn't see Reese at Jude's.

Thump. Thump. Thump.

"Fitz!"

It's been a *looong* day.

Her momma gave her a bell to use to call for one of us if she needs something. I hid it away an hour ago and now she's resorted to banging on the walls.

Every time I try to talk to Abby about the accident, and what Reese said, she avoids the conversation. First, she had a headache and couldn't talk. Then she had a coughing fit and needed water and couldn't speak for an hour. Then the last time I tried when her parents were out of the room, she faked sleep.

She is feeling better and clearly milking it for all she's worth, and I'm about to lose my shit.

Reese was right. I'm falling into Abby's old manipulative ways. She's dragging her injuries out, playing the *woe is me* card over and over again, and using me to hide everything from her parents.

Thump. Thump. Thump.

With a sigh, I go to the kitchen for a glass to bring to the princess upstairs.

She's being extra bratty because her momma went to the store to buy her more magazines—since she ran out—and her dad's at work, so she knows I'm the only one who can respond.

I need to tell her parents the truth about our relationship, or lack thereof. But the few times I've mustered up the courage to say something, Martha looks at me with those wide eyes. The same ones I've known my whole life and I falter and change the subject.

But I can't go on like this anymore.

And honestly, neither can Abby. She needs help, more than what I can give.

I hate lying. I hate not talking to Reese like I want to. I can't even imagine what she's feeling. When I think about how I would feel if she had to pretend to be with Duke or something, my heart breaks all over again.

It's Sunday, and Jude agreed to hold off the final Bedlam event until Tuesday, which would be exactly two weeks from when we held the first event. But I need to see Reese long before then. I need to get Abby to tell her folks the truth, and quick.

Inside Abby's bedroom—still set up like it was before we went off to college, with her four-post bed and fluffy white comforter and pink carpet—I set the glass on her bedside table. Her face must feel better since her volume has increased, but it still looks terrible, dark-purple splotches mixed with mottled shades of yellow and green.

"Thanks, sweetie." She takes a sip from the cup and sets it back down delicately. "Will you get me the nail polish from over there, too?" She points a languid finger to the white vanity.

I hand it to her. "I'm not your sweetie, Abby. And we need to talk about your accident."

She grimaces. "You know, now isn't a great time. Maybe tomorrow." She opens her nail polish and starts painting her toes.

Her tone is flippant. Dismissive. Like now she's got her nail polish and she's done with me and the complete lack of caring about anything but herself snaps something inside of me.

"No, Abby. We're talking about it now."

She rolls her eyes. "Don't be so dramatic."

"I'm the dramatic one?" I think my head might pop off I'm so angry. "I refuse to be held hostage by you forever. You will tell me what really happened and why you crashed into that tree."

Her eyes fill with tears. "I'm still recovering. My parents have already been through so much. How can you do this to them?" She weeps quietly into her hands, but it doesn't sway me.

"How can I . . . Do you even hear yourself?" I'm about to tell her to cut the crap, but the front door opens and her momma calls out she's home. "Look. Here's how this is going down. You're gonna tell me the truth, right now, or I'll tell your parents everything I know, with or without you."

"You wouldn't," she says through sobs.

"Watch me." I make for the door.

"Wait!" she calls when I'm halfway out.

I face her, crossing my arms over my chest, standing near the door.

"Okay, okay." She moves her hands away and her eyes are clear and sharp and I'm stunned all over again that I fell for her lies for so long. "You're right, Fitz. I might have gone off the road on purpose, but I didn't want to hurt myself. I wasn't going fast at all, but then it was dark and the shoulder was steeper than I thought. It was just because you weren't calling me back and I wanted to show you how much I still care about you. I did it for you, don't you see?"

I think I've passed the point of disbelief and gone straight into flabbergast. I can't even speak, and I don't have to because Abby keeps going.

"You don't understand. I can't tell them about what I've done and Kevin and everything . . . everything I did to you. I can't stand it. They'll hate me."

"They won't hate you." *Though I might.* I sigh and run a frustrated hand through my hair. I'm surprised I'm not bald after the last two days. "How's this. We tell them we mutually decided we're better as friends. It's not a lie, that's why we broke up. I'll leave out the cheating and fake accident and let you to decide if and when you want to tell them anything else. But I'm done with this. I can't keep lying to my parents. I'm with Reese now." I hold her gaze so she knows I mean it.

She crosses her arms over her chest. "I can't believe you moved on so fast," she grumbles.

"You moved on faster."

"That doesn't count. Kevin was . . . a blip." She flicks a finger at me. "You won't have a blip, Fitz. You stick."

I think about Reese. Her funny faces, her quick brain, and the way she felt in my arms. "I sure hope so."

"I can't pretend to be happy for you."

"You get to feel however you feel."

All I'm feeling is relief.

Until fifteen minutes later, when we've broken the news to her momma.

She cries, like I knew she would, and she wants more

details than I'm prepared to give, but Abby finally convinces her we decided we were better as friends.

I throw into the conversation that Abby needs help—really needs to talk to someone about her accident. Abby protests, but I think Martha listens, at least.

I've done all I can do.

And after all of that, after weeks of lying and drama and angst . . . it's all over in a matter of minutes with one short—albeit difficult—conversation.

Once I escape, I immediately try to reach Reese, but her phone is still going to voice mail.

When I pull up at Jude's, she's not there.

Her car is gone, and inside, her clothes aren't hanging in the closet and her box of favorite books is gone.

And of course, the first person I run into is Beast.

"Where is she?"

He shrugs his giant shoulders and I groan in frustration. Why am I asking him? I may as well ask Mr. Bojangles.

I find Jude in the backyard, cat in his lap, reading a romance novel.

"Where is she?"

"I believe our little Ms. Tootsie Roll has made her way back to the homestead."

"But there's still one more challenge to go."

"There is. One final challenge and the announcement of the big winner Tuesday night. She already said she would be here for it." He languidly turns the page.

How can he be so blasé about this?

"If she doesn't show, the room is yours," he adds, like that's what I want to hear. "Although I hope she shows. I've got a lot of money riding on this."

The room might be mine. It was all I wanted. But now it's not what I want at all.

And since Reese won't answer her phone, I'll have to go to her.

Ten minutes later, I'm heading down the long drive, kicking up gravel as I speed my way to the Jackson ranch.

I come to a halt behind Reese's VW and jump out of my truck, but I don't make it very far.

"Can I help you?" Granny's standing at the top of the patio steps with an ancient break-action shotgun.

I hold up my hands. "Can I speak with Reese, please?"

"Don't you think if she wanted to talk to you, she'd answer her phone?"

"I reckon that's true, but it doesn't mean I'm gonna give up easy, ma'am."

"And why's that?"

"Reese means a lot to me. I'd face down this shotgun right here if it meant I could talk to her, even only for a minute."

Her eyes squint at me, her face a blank mask.

"Tootsie Roll!" she yells so suddenly I startle. "You wanna hear what this here young gent has to say?"

"No!" The shout comes from above the porch and I step back to eye the next floor.

There's an open window, pale curtains blowing in the breeze.

"I know you hate me right now, but can we please talk?" I call out.

There's a long moment of silence. Reese doesn't appear in the window. Granny caresses the trigger of her shotgun and squints harder.

Finally, Reese's voice calls out. "Have you told your parents about Abby yet?"

I swear softly.

"That sounds like a no to me." Granny cocks the hammer.

"Now just hold on a minute there." I lift my hands again. "I've told Abby's parents. I haven't had a chance to talk to my own folks yet. But I will, I promise. I'll go over there right after I leave here. If I get to leave alive," I add.

Granny flashes her teeth in what might be a smile but also could be a snarl.

More silence, and then Reese speaks, but I have to strain to catch all the words because she's not yelling anymore.

"What if they don't want to meet me? They probably love Abby. She's the one they've thought you would be with forever."

My heart wrenches at the softly spoken words, words laced with an uncertainty I helped create. Reese has struggled with fitting in her whole life, and now I've put her in this position . . . "I don't care what they think."

"I do. Family matters to both of us."

"I think my parents will love you just as much as I do."

More silence at that pronouncement, but Granny

does point the gun down at the ground, so it feels like a small victory.

"Will you at least show up for the final challenge?" I call out.

It takes a few long seconds, but then there is an answer on the breeze. A tentative one. "Maybe."

"What happened to not giving up?"

Silence.

Granny lifts the gun again.

"All right, all right. I'm leaving, but I'm not finished. Please show up Tuesday night, Reese. You have all of tomorrow to think it over. That's all I ask."

I IMMEDIATELY DRIVE HOME AND GIVE THE NEWS TO MY parents. Momma already heard from Martha, so it's not much of a surprise.

What is a surprise is the big hug she gives me.

"You know we love Abby, but I've long suspected she's not the one for you."

Of all the surprises I've been dealt today, it's a small one in comparison, but it still takes me aback. "You have?"

"Of course, baby. She's a bit unsteady. You need someone more independent like yourself. Someone who will make you happy and will push you in ways that help you grow, not hold you back." Momma meets my eyes square on. "Does this girl do that for you?"

A slow smile spreads my face. "She does."

"Then that's all I can ask for. Along with some help for Abby. Do you think she'll talk to someone about her troubles?"

"I'm not sure. I can only hope."

I finally head back to Jude's as the sun is setting and find him still reading out on the back porch.

Plopping on the chair in front of him, I lean forward with elbows on my knees. "I really screwed up with Reese. I need to fix it."

His eyes don't leave his book. "Is that right?" he murmurs.

"I need your help."

Now his gaze lifts to mine. "What did you have in mind?"

"It has to be big. A romantic gesture." Sudden hope lifts my mood. Jude loves romance. "Got any ideas?"

"You could go to her house with a boom box. Blast some Peter Gabriel in front of her door."

I shake my head. "That's lame. And Granny might shoot me. I need a chance to see her and talk to her, explain myself and apologize. You know, really grovel."

He pets Mr. Bojangles with one hand. "Ride up on a white horse to her little dive apartment and rescue her. Or, you know, a stretch limo. And then she can rescue you right back."

I frown. Is he even listening? "She doesn't have an apartment. And where would I get a limo?"

He snaps. "I've got it. Tell her parents, *no one puts baby in the corner.*"

I roll my eyes but can't keep the laugh from escaping.

"Is this really all you have? Stuff from bad eighties rom coms?"

"What else is there?"

"I need to show her I choose her. That I'll always choose her. And I need to do it in a big way."

He puts the book down and sits up, leaning toward me. "And how exactly did you want to do it, Casanova?"

"I might have an idea. But I'll need your help."

24

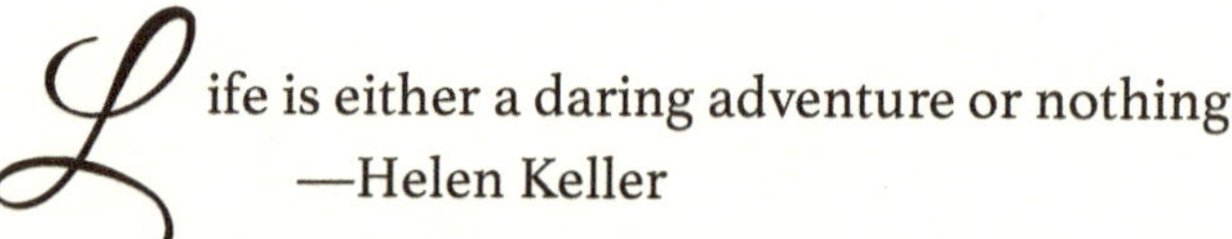

Life is either a daring adventure or nothing.
—Helen Keller

Reese

In the end, I almost don't go to the last Bedlam event, but then I realize I want to. I have to.

Not because Fitz asked—even though I have to admit he's a big draw—but also because I'm not an ostrich anymore. I won't hide with my head in the sand. Which actually isn't an accurate description, because the ostrich merely digs holes for its nests and then they stick their heads in several times a day to turn their eggs, making it appear they are hiding— But I digress.

It's nearly six and surprisingly quiet when I pull up

at Jude's. No extra cars out front or people milling about like normal.

Inside, the house is quiet and empty.

"Hello?"

"Out back," Jude calls.

He's in the backyard. Alone.

"Where is everyone?" I ask.

He smiles and lifts his megaphone. "Welcome to the final round of Bedlam!"

"Ugh." I cover my ears. "It's just me. And we're like three feet apart, you turd."

His grin widens and then he leans forward and hands me a folded piece of white paper. "This is for you."

I give him a questioning look, but he says nothing, so I take the paper and open it.

You will find the first clue in the building with the most stories in every town you go.

I meet Jude's eyes. "What is this?"

"The final game. A treasure hunt."

"Where's Fitz?" I glance around the empty yard, but he's not hiding in the hedges. "Did he already start?"

"You'll have to find out for yourself, babies."

"This better be a fair competition, Jude."

"It will be, Tootsie Roll, I promise. Now go solve the first riddle to find out where to go next."

I roll my eyes and lift the paper. "This is child's play. It's clearly the library."

"Then you better get on it."

I frown at him, but what else can I do? I'm not gonna

argue. So I leave Jude and the house behind and go to the library.

Once I get there, I realize I have no idea where to look for the next clue.

Quite a few students are making use of the desks set up for study sessions, talking quietly or working on laptops. No one is paying me any mind.

Except for Beast, who is standing at the information desk.

“What are you doing? Do you work here?” I ask, not really expecting a response.

And I don’t get one. At least, not a verbal one.

Beast hands me a book.

It’s my book. The one I lent Fitz. *Northanger Abbey*.

A piece of paper flutters to the ground when I open the front cover.

I pick it up.

You will find your next clue where it all began, where cups of pens fly and bulletin boards stand vacant, but no longer.

The housing office. The next clue must be on the board. Are they even open now?

I glance up to see if I can get anything out of Beast—even a nonverbal cue might be helpful—but he’s gone.

And before I can question why I’m continuing this game, which has clearly been arranged by Fitz, not Jude, my feet carry me out of the library and toward the housing office. I want to see where this whole thing leads.

The housing office is empty—they close at four and

it's nearly six—but the door is unlocked when I push it open. There's a flyer attached to the board with a pin.

I can be found in a pen, but I am not ink. I am named after a perennial plant and was forced to wear a dress.

Begonia. I pull out the pin and examine it. It's an old Victorian style hatpin, all gleaming silver with a small pink rose at the top. I leave the office with a smile, remembering to pull the door on my way out instead of push.

The pen outside the barn is empty; Begonia must be off somewhere else for the evening. But wrapped around the fence is something colorful. I unwrap the item. It's a canvas bag tie-dyed in bright colors. Words on the side read, *I like big books and I cannot lie.*

I pull it off the fence and open it up. Inside is the next clue.

I am flora not fauna, I am shrubbery not grass. You'll thank me not to mention you and this word in the same sentence. Find your next clue under my foliage to the northeast.

I laugh. The bushes. Back at Jude's? Must be in the northeast corner of the yard. And now I have a bag to put all the clues and items I've gathered. How very useful.

He remembered.

Ten minutes later, I'm walking back into Jude's. It's empty.

In the backyard, in the northeast corner, there's a present. It's wrapped in Christmas paper.

Excitement flickers through me and I rip it open.

Inside is a can of Spam, which makes me chuckle, along with the next clue.

Some take me in the morning, some take me in the evening, but I never actually leave.

The shower.

It doesn't escape me that Fitz is leading me to all the places we spent time together. And giving me presents to show he listened. And he cares.

In the shower, there's another Christmas present. I tear it open to find another old book. *Pride and Prejudice.* Not a first edition, but inside he's written a quote from the book along with the clue.

I cannot fix on the hour, or the spot, or the look, or the words, which laid the foundation. I was in the middle before I knew that I had begun.

I blink away tears. It's from the final scene, when Mr. Darcy once again declares his intentions for Elizabeth Bennet.

Mr. Fitzwilliam Darcy, to be precise.

I read the next clue.

I have four legs, one head, and a foot. And twinkle lights overhead. I also rhyme with head. And I don't mean that in a dirty way. But maybe I do.

I laugh and then take a deep breath, before walking down the hall to the room. The door is shut. I'm so nervous my palms are sweating. I can't breathe properly. I gulp in some air before pushing the door open.

Fitz is there, alone, dressed in a grey button-up shirt and dark jeans.

His smile is hopeful and tentative. He's holding a small, wrapped box.

I'm still clutching my bag with all of the papers, *Northanger Abbey*, the Spam, and the hatpin inside, *Pride and Prejudice* in the other hand.

"You came."

"How did you know I'd get to the end?" I ask.

His smile is tentative. "I knew you wouldn't give up."

"Risky."

"It's how I roll." And then we stare at each other for long seconds before he startles and holds out the box in his hand, wrapped in Santa-covered paper. "This is for you."

I can't take it though. My hands are full. I hold the items up a little and it's like he's just now realized I'm holding all of these things.

"Oh." He puts the box down on the bed, then takes everything from me and puts it all on the dresser and his hands are shaking a little and he's *nervous*.

He's nervous about *me*.

The idea is so startling and thrilling, I laugh out loud.

"Are you laughing at me?" His playful tone belies the hurt words, his eyes crinkling with mirth.

"Yes. I am."

My hands are finally free and he hands me the little box. "Here."

I tear it open. It's a small jewelry box.

My eyes fly to his, brows lifting.

"That's not what you think it is. I mean, we're a little

young for what you're thinking, but I won't take it off the table for some time in the future."

Heart thumping, palms clammy with nerves, I open the little box and laugh.

It's the key.

I hold it up and meet Fitz's eyes, which are gazing back at me, both hopeful and a little uncertain.

"I'm so sorry about everything," he says. "But everyone knows the full truth now. And I want to take you home to meet my parents before they leave for Florida. I already told them all about you and they want to meet you too."

"They're not upset about Abby?"

"Not at all. I mean, they're upset Abby's not doing well, but when I told Momma I had a new girl, she said, 'Praise the Lord!' And then she said she was happier than a mule in a pickle patch."

I laugh, my heart lifting with his words, easing some of my anxiety. "She was happy you and Abby are over?"

"Apparently she's had some concerns about Abby for a while."

"Sounds like a common theme," I say with a grimace.

"I don't want to talk about her anymore. I want to talk about us. Can you forgive me?"

"You gave me a book," I say. "Of course I can forgive you."

He whoops and then I'm in his arms, his mouth on mine, lingering for a moment before we separate long enough for him to say, "You know, if I have to buy you a book every time I screw up, you're gonna need a bigger box."

I laugh and then we're kissing again and my hands thread through his hair, but the key gets tangled in it too.

I pull back far enough to hold the key between us. "Does this mean we're going to share the room?"

He rubs the back of his neck with one hand, keeping the other around my waist. "No. I wouldn't put you in that position. I'm moving in with Annabel. She found an apartment, but she needs a roommate. It won't be till next month but I can sleep on the couch till then." He shrugs. "It doesn't matter to me."

"So, this means I've won?" I can't stop smiling.

"I think it means we both have."

THE END

ABOUT THE AUTHOR

Go here to sign up for the newsletter! www.authormaryframe.com

Mary Frame is a full-time mother and wife with a full-time job. She has no idea how she manages to write novels except that it helps being a dedicated introvert. She doesn't enjoy writing about herself in third person, but she does enjoy reading, writing, dancing, and damaging the eardrums of her coworkers when she randomly decides to sing to them. She lives in Reno, Nevada, with her husband, two children, and a border collie named Stella.

She LOVES hearing from readers and will not only respond but likely begin stalking them while tossing out hearts and flowers and rainbows! If that doesn't creep you out, email her at:
maryframeauthor@gmail.com
Follow her on Twitter: @marewulf
Like her Facebook author page: www.facebook.com/AuthorMaryFrame

Imperfect Series reading order:

Book One: Imperfect Chemistry
Book Two: Imperfectly Criminal
Book Three: Practically Imperfect
Book Four: Picture Imperfect
Book Five: Imperfect Strangers
Book Six: Imperfectly Delicious

The Dorky Duet (Plus a companion novel!)
Rirdorkulous
Geektastic
Nerdelicious

The Extraordinary Series
Anything But Extraordinary
A Life Less Extraordinary
Extraordinary World

Coming June 2021, a brand new rom com series!
Time of My Life